영미 명작 단편선

영국편

영미 명작 단편선 – 영국편

초판 1쇄 펴낸날 | 2019년 1월 21일

편저자 | 김보원
펴낸이 | 류수노
펴낸곳 | (사)한국방송통신대학교출판문화원
　　　　03088 서울시 종로구 이화장길 54
　　　　대표전화 1644-1232
　　　　팩스 02-741-4570
　　　　홈페이지 http://press.knou.ac.kr
　　　　출판등록 1982년 6월 7일 제1-491호

출판위원장 | 장종수
편집 | 신경진 · 명수경
본문 디자인 | (주)성지이디피
표지 디자인 | 이상선

ⓒ 김보원, 2019
ISBN 978-89-20-99239-1 93840

값 10,000원

이 도서의 국립중앙도서관 출판예정도서목록(CIP)은 서지정보유통지원시스템 홈페이지(http://seoji.nl.go.kr)와
국가자료공동목록시스템(http://www.nl.go.kr/kolisnet)에서 이용하실 수 있습니다.(CIP제어번호: CIP2019001163)

영미 명작 단편선

영국편

김보원 편저

에피스테메
EPISTEME

영미 명작 단편선 – 영국편

차 례 ⋘

책을 펴내며

이 책은 영국 단편소설을 원문으로 직접 읽으며 감상하기를 원하는 독자들을 위해 펴낸 책이다. 단편소설이 본격적으로 꽃을 피우기 시작한 20세기에 발표된 대표적인 명작 단편소설 8편을 선정하였고, 본문 하단에 최소한의 주석을 붙여서 일정 수준의 영어 독해 능력을 갖춘 독자라면 혼자서 작품을 감상하기에 어려움이 없게 하였다. 아울러 작품 말미에는 작품 감상에 핵심 요건이 되는 주제를 중심으로 두세 쪽 분량의 작품 해설이 덧붙여 있어서 작품 감상을 위한 가이드 역할을 할 수 있을 것이다.

수록 작품 중에는 "The Luncheon"이나 "The Ant and the Grasshopper" 처럼 앉은 자리에서 바로 읽어낼 수 있는 깔끔한 길이의 작품도 있지만, "Half-Holiday"나 "The Rocking-Horse Winner"처럼 긴 호흡으로 공을 들여야 완독에 이를 수 있는 작품들도 함께 실려 있다. 아울러 주제적인 측면에서도 스냅 사진처럼 인상적인 한 장면에 인물과 사건의 모든 것이 압축된 가벼운 작품이 있는 반면에, 표면의 스토리를 넘어 이면의 역사와 문화에 대한 탐구를 통해 더 깊이 있는 이해가 가능해지는 무거운 작품도 있다. 따라서 수록된 8편의 작품을 차례대로 읽을

필요는 없으므로 자신의 기호와 흥미, 시간에 따라 골라 읽는 것도 요령이다.

　책의 제목에서 보듯이 이 책의 자매편인 『영미 명작 단편선-미국편』의 출간이 곧 이어질 예정이므로 관심 있는 독자들은 두 책을 통해 영국과 미국의 대표적 단편소설을 한꺼번에 감상하는 계획을 세워볼 수도 있겠다. 이 책들은 방송대 프라임칼리지에서 운영하는 두 편의 교양강좌 "원어로 읽는 영미 명작 단편선"의 교재로도 사용하고 있으므로, 작품 감상을 넘어 본격적인 학습을 원하는 독자들은 이 강의를 적극 활용해 보는 것도 좋을 것이다.

– 편저자 김보원

영미 명작 단편선_1

The Luncheon

William Somerset Maugham

William Somerset Maugham(1874~1965)은 20세기 전반에
활동한 영국 소설가로, 대표작으로는 자전적 소설인 *Of Human
Bondage*(1915)와 화가 고갱의 삶을 모델로 한 *The Moon and
Sixpence*(1919) 등이 있다. 하지만 Maugham의 소설적 재능
은 장편소설보다 단편소설에서 더 뛰어나다는 평가를 받고
있으며, 그 평가에 걸맞은 많은 수작을 발견할 수 있다. "The
Luncheon"(1924)은 길이는 짧지만 영미 단편소설선에 빠지지
않고 수록될 만큼 유명한 작품으로, 가난한 청년작가의 허영심
을 소재로 인간 본성의 한 단면을 작가 특유의 아이러니와 유머
로 재현해 내는 데 성공하고 있다.

The Luncheon

»–

I caught sight of[1] her at the play and in answer to her
beckoning I went over during the interval and sat down
beside her. It was long since I had last seen her and if someone
had not mentioned her name I hardly think I would have
⁵ recognised her. She addressed me brightly.

"Well, it's many years since we first met. How time does fly!
We're none of us getting any younger.[2] Do you remember the
first time I saw you? You asked me to luncheon."

Did I remember?

¹⁰ It was twenty years ago and I was living in Paris. I had a
tiny apartment in the Latin Quarter[3] overlooking a cemetery
and I was earning barely enough money to keep body and

---

1 catch sight of: 발견하다, 흘끗 보다
2 none of us getting any younger : 누구도 젊어지는 법은 없지요
3 the Latin Quarter: 라텡 지구 *파리의 주요 대학들이 위치한 대학가로, 중
   세시대부터 대학이 있었고 따라서 이 지역에서는 라틴어가 통용되었기 때문
   에 이렇게 불림.

soul together.[4] She had read a book of mine and had written to me about it. I answered, thanking her, and presently I received from her another letter saying that she was passing through Paris and would like to have a chat with me; but her time was limited and the only free moment she had was on the following Thursday; she was spending the morning at the Luxembourg and would I give her a little luncheon at Foyot's afterwards? Foyot's is a restaurant at which the French senators eat and it was so far beyond my means[5] that I had never even thought of going there. But I was flattered and I was too young to have learned to say no to a woman. (Few men, I may add, learn this until they are too old to make it of any consequence to a woman what they say.)[6] I had eighty francs (gold francs) to last me the rest of the month and a modest luncheon should not cost more than fifteen. If I cut out[7] coffee for the next two weeks I could manage well enough.

---

4 to keep body and soul together : 겨우 생계를 유지하다
5 beyond my means : 내 (경제적) 능력을 벗어나는
6 Few men learn ... what they say : 남자들은 자기가 하는 말이 여자들한테 아무 의미가 없을 만큼 늙어서야 겨우 이것을 깨닫는다
7 cut out : =stop eating or drinking something (usually to improve your health)

I answered that I would meet my friend — by correspondence[8] — at Foyot's on Thursday at half-past twelve. She was not so young as I expected and in appearance imposing[9] rather than attractive. She was in fact a woman of forty (a charming age, but not one that excites a sudden and devastating passion at first sight),[10] and she gave me the impression of having more teeth, white and large and even, than were necessary for any practical purpose. She was talkative, but since she seemed inclined to talk about me I was prepared to be an attentive listener.

I was startled when the bill of fare[11] was brought, for the prices were a great deal higher than I had anticipated. But she reassured me.

"I never eat anything for luncheon," she said.

"Oh, don't say that!" I answered generously.

"I never eat more than one thing. I think people eat far too much nowadays. A little fish, perhaps. I wonder if they have

---

8 my friend — by correspondence : 편지로 만들어진 — 내 친구
9 imposing : 당당한, 눈길을 끄는
10 one that excites ... at first sight : 첫눈에 갑자기 엄청난 사랑을 촉발시키는 나이
11 the bill of fare : 메뉴

any salmon."

Well, it was early in the year for salmon and it was not on the bill of fare, but I asked the waiter if there was any. Yes, a beautiful salmon had just come in, it was the first they had had. I ordered it for my guest. The waiter asked her if she would have something while it was being cooked.

"No," she answered, "I never eat more than one thing. Unless you had a little caviare. I never mind caviare."

My heart sank a little. I knew I could not afford caviare, but I could not very well tell her that. I told the waiter by all means[12] to bring caviare. For myself I chose the cheapest dish on the menu and that was a mutton chop.[13]

"I think you're unwise to eat meat," she said. "I don't know how you can expect to work after eating heavy things like chops. I don't believe in[14] overloading my stomach."

Then came the question of drink.

"I never drink anything for luncheon," she said.

"Neither do I," I answered promptly.

"Except white wine," she proceeded as though I had not

---

12 by all means : =in any way possible, regardless of risk or expense

13 chop : (양고기·돼지고기의) 갈빗살 한 토막

14 believe in : ~이 옳다고(좋다고) 생각하다

spoken. "These French white wines are so light. They're wonderful for the digestion."

"What would you like?" I asked, hospitable still, but not exactly effusive.[15]

She gave me a bright and amicable flash of her white teeth.

"My doctor won't let me drink anything but champagne."

I fancy I turned a trifle pale. I ordered half a bottle. I mentioned casually[16] that my doctor had absolutely forbidden me to drink champagne.

"What are you going to drink, then?"

"Water."

She ate the caviare and she ate the salmon. She talked gaily of art and literature and music. But I wondered what the bill would come to.[17] When my mutton chop arrived she took me quite seriously to task.[18]

"I see that you're in the habit of eating a heavy luncheon. I'm sure it's a mistake. Why don't you follow my example and just eat one thing? I'm sure you'd feel ever so much better for it."

---

15 effusive : (감정 표현이) 야단스러운, 과장된
16 casually : 불쑥, 아무 생각 없이
17 come to : (총계가) ~이 되다
18 took me quite seriously to task : 무척 심하게 나를 질책했다

"I am only going to eat one thing," I said, as the waiter came again with the bill of fare.

She waved him aside with an airy gesture.[19]

"No, no, I never eat anything for luncheon. Just a bite, I never want more than that, and I eat that more as an excuse 5 for conversation than anything else.[20] I couldn't possibly eat anything more — unless they had some of those giant asparagus. I should be sorry to leave Paris without having some of them."

My heart sank. I had seen them in the shops and I knew that 10 they were horribly expensive. My mouth had often watered[21] at the sight of them.

"Madame wants to know if you have any of those giant asparagus," I asked the waiter.

I tried with all my might[22] to will[23] him to say no. A happy 15

---

19 waved him aside with an airy gesture : 그를 대수롭지 않게 여기며 물러나라고 손짓을 했다 ＊wave aside : =direct someone or something to stand aside by or as if by waving the hand or arm

20 more as an excuse for conversation than anything else : 무엇보다도 대화를 하기 위한 구실로

21 water : 침이 괴다, 군침이 돌다

22 with all my might : 전력을 다해

23 will : 의지력을 발휘하다, 애를 쓰다

smile spread over his broad, priest-like face, and he assured me that they had some so large, so splendid, so tender, that it was a marvel.

"I'm not in the least hungry," my guest sighed, "but if you insist I don't mind having some asparagus."

I ordered them.

"Aren't you going to have any?"

"No, I never eat asparagus."

"I know there are people who don't like them. The fact is, you ruin your palate by all the meat you eat."

We waited for the asparagus to be cooked. Panic seized me. It was not a question now of how much money I should have left over for the rest of the month, but whether I had enough to pay the bill. It would be mortifying[24] to find myself ten francs short[25] and be obliged to borrow from my guest. I could not bring myself to do that. I knew exactly how much I had and if the bill came to more, I had made up my mind that I would put my hand in my pocket and with a dramatic

---

24 mortifying: 분한, 원통한, 창피한 * mortify: 굴욕감을 주다, 몹시 당황하게 하다

25 short: =lacking in length or amount

cry start up[26] and say it had been picked. Of course it would be awkward if she had not money enough either to pay the bill. Then the only thing would be to leave my watch and say I would come back and pay later.

The asparagus appeared. They were enormous, succulent, and appetising. The smell of the melted butter tickled my nostrils as the nostrils of Jehovah were tickled by the burned offerings[27] of the virtuous Semites.[28] I watched the abandoned[29] woman thrust them down her throat in large voluptuous mouthfuls and in my polite way I discoursed on the condition of the drama in the Balkans. At last she finished.

"Coffee?" I said.

"Yes, just an ice-cream and coffee," she answered.

I was past caring now[30], so I ordered coffee for myself and an ice-cream and coffee for her.

"You know, there's one thing I thoroughly believe in," she

---

26 start up : 벌떡 일어나다 *cf.* When the alarm rang, I started up.

27 the burned offerings : 번제물(燔祭物) *번제 : 짐승을 통째로 태워 제물로 바친 제사

28 the virtuous Semites : 선량한 셈족 *여호와(Jehovah)께 제사를 드리던 구약성서의 이스라엘 민족을 가리킴.

29 abandoned : 파렴치한, 통제불능의

30 I was past caring now : 이제는 전혀 신경이 쓰이지 않았다

said, as she ate the ice-cream. "One should always get up from a meal feeling one could eat a little more."

"Are you still hungry?" I asked faintly.

"Oh, no, I'm not hungry; you see, I don't eat luncheon. I have a cup of coffee in the morning and then dinner, but I never eat more than one thing for luncheon. I was speaking for you."

"Oh, I see!"

Then a terrible thing happened. While we were waiting for the coffee, the head waiter, with an ingratiating[31] smile on his false face,[32] came up to us bearing a large basket full of huge peaches. They had the blush of an innocent girl; they had the rich tone of an Italian landscape.[33] But surely peaches were not in season then? Lord knew what they cost. I knew too — a little later, for my guest, going on with her conversation, absentmindedly took one.

"You see, you've filled your stomach with a lot of meat" — my one miserable little chop — "and you can't eat any more. But I've just had a snack and I shall enjoy a peach."

---

31 ingratiating : 알랑거리는, 환심을 사려는
32 false face : 꾸며 낸 얼굴 *원래 false face는 '탈, 가면'을 가리킴.
33 an Italian landscape : 이탈리아 풍경화

The bill came and when I paid it I found that I had only enough for a quite inadequate tip. Her eyes rested for an instant on the three francs I left for the waiter and I knew that she thought me mean. But when I walked out of the restaurant I had the whole month before me and not a penny in my pocket.

"Follow my example," she said as we shook hands, "and never eat more than one thing for luncheon."

"I'll do better than that," I retorted. "I'll eat nothing for dinner to-night."

"Humorist!" she cried gaily, jumping into a cab. "You're quite a humorist!"

But I have had my revenge[34] at last. I do not believe that I am a vindictive man, but when the immortal gods take a hand[35] in the matter it is pardonable to observe the result with complacency. Today she weighs twenty-one stone.[36]

---

34 have one's revenge : 복수하다
35 take a hand : 관여하다, 개입하다
36 stone : 스톤 ＊옛날 무게 단위로 약 14파운드에 해당함.

작품 해설

1. 아이러니

이 작품을 읽는 가장 큰 즐거움은 아이러니(irony)라는 한 단어로 요약된다. 가난한 청년작가의 주머니 사정은 아랑곳하지 않고 코스 요리를 마구 먹어 대는 중년 여성은 뻔뻔하게도 입으로는 계속해서 "점심에는 아무것도 안 먹어요."(I never eat anything for luncheon.)라고 둘러댄다. 엄청난 양의 식사를 하고도 간식(snack)을 먹었다고 태연하게 말하는 여성, 입으로 하는 말과 몸으로 하는 행동의 불일치에서 비롯되는 이 여성의 후안무치, 표리부동에 대한 풍자가 이 작품을 읽는 가장 큰 즐거움이다. 물론 "오늘 그녀의 체중은 21스톤이었다."(Today she weights twenty-one stone.)로 마무리되는 작품의 종결부는 그 풍자가 예리한 칼날처럼 사람을 찌르고 공격하는 풍자라기보다 유쾌한 웃음을 수반하는 해학적 풍자에 가깝다는 것을 말해 준다.

이와 같이 말과 행동의 모순, 외양과 실체의 괴리, 의도와 결과의 불일치 등에서 만들어지는 문학적 효과를 뭉뚱그려서 아이러니라고 한다. 이를테면 정직하고 성실한 노력 끝에 '운명의 장난'처럼 찾아온 비극적 결과라거나, 테베에 창궐한 역병의 근원을 찾아간 오이디푸스 왕이 끝내 그 근원이 자신이라는 진실과 조우할 수밖에 없는 안타까운 상황 또한 아이러니에 해당한다. 흔히 기구한 운명이나 뜻밖의 사건 전개를 가리킬 때 사용하는 '운명의 장난'을 영어로 표현할 때도 'the irony of fate'라고 한다.

유감스럽게도 아이러니의 우리말 역어는 아직 확정되어 있지 않아서 '아이러니', '아이러니한'(ironic)으로 표기하여 쓰고 있다. 기존 용어로는 '반어법'이 아이러니와 가장 가까운 수사법이라고 볼 수 있지만, 이 경우 언어표현과 지칭하는 내용의 불일치를 가리키는 '언어적 아이러니'(verbal irony)를 가리킨다는 점에서 영어의 아이러니가 지닌 함의의 일부에 불과하다.

2. the abandoned woman?

이 작품을 읽는 또 하나의 재미는 주인공으로부터 "파렴치한"(abandoned) 인물로 비난받는 여성이 과연 그런 비난을 받아 마땅한가 하는 점이다. 요컨대 이 여성이 가난한 청년작가를 등쳐 먹기 위해 의도적으로 접근한 것인지 아닌지가 분명치 않기 때문이다. 편견을 버리고 작품을 꼼꼼히 다시 읽어 보면, 여성의 행동은 포요(Foyot's) 식당에서 그 정도의 식사를 '가볍게' 하는 상류층의 여성이라면 충분히 있을법한 일상으로 이해할 수 있고, 따라서 여성을 '파렴치범'으로 모는 것은 온당치 않다. 이와 같은 판단의 근거는 무엇보다도 이 작품의 서술이 바로 당사자인 청년작가의 1인칭 시점으로 전개된다는 데 있다. 말하자면 그는 사건의 이해당사자이며, 따라서 그의 서술을 전적으로 신뢰할 수 있는가 하는 문제는 따져 보아야 하기 때문이다. 비평용어로 옮기자면 그는 '신뢰할 수 없는 서술자'(the unreliable narrator)에 해당하는 것이다.

그런 점에서 이 단편의 실질적인 초점은 중년의 여성독자가 아니라 서술자인 작가('I')로 옮기는 것이 자연스러워 보인다. 여성의 의도가 무엇인가는 '열린 결말'(the open ending)로 남겨 두고, 이야기의 실질적인 초점을 서술자의 자기이해(self-knowledge)로 이전하자는 것이다. 논란의 여지없이 분명한 사실은 청년작가가 여성의 편지를 받고 허영심이 발동하였다는 것이며, 그 당시에는 "너무 어려서 여성에게 '아니요'라고 말할 줄을 몰랐다"고 후일의 서술자가 솔직하게 고백하고 있기 때문이다. 이후의 전개에서도 결국 스토리 전개의 핵심은 여성의 파렴치함이라기보다, 우쭐함에서 시작하여 놀람, 당황, 체념, 분노로 이어지는 서술자의 심리 변화 과정으로 이해하는 것이 이 작품에 대한 훨씬 온당한 평가일 것이다.

영미 명작 단편선_2

A Cup of Tea

Katherine Mansfield

Katherine Mansfield(1888~1923)는 뉴질랜드 출신으로 영국에서 활동한 독특한 이력의 소설가이다. 식민지 뉴질랜드의 유복한 가문에서 태어난 덕분에 유럽에서 교육을 받을 수 있었고 이후 작품활동은 주로 영국에서 하다가 35세의 나이로 요절한 작가이다. 장편소설보다는 단편소설에서 재능을 발휘하였으며, 주로 여성적 감수성, 여성 심리에 대한 섬세한 관찰이 돋보이는 작품을 많이 남겼다. "Bliss"(1918), "Miss Brill"(1920), "The Garden Party"(1922) 등의 대표작이 있으며, 여기 수록한 "A Cup of Tea"(1922)는 겨울날 오후 런던을 배경으로 상류층 여성과 거지소녀의 특별한 만남을 통해 여성 심리의 독특한 단면을 예리하게 포착해 낸 작품이다.

A Cup of Tea

Rosemary Fell was not exactly beautiful. No, you couldn't have called her beautiful. Pretty? Well, if you took her to pieces....[1] But why be so cruel as to take anyone to pieces? She was young, brilliant, extremely modern, exquisitely well dressed, amazingly well read in the newest of the new books, and her parties were the most delicious[2] mixture of the really important people and... artists — quaint creatures,[3] discoveries of hers,[4] some of them too terrifying for words, but others quite presentable[5] and amusing.

Rosemary had been married two years. She had a duck of a boy.[6] No, not Peter — Michael. And her husband absolutely

---

1 take ~ to pieces : ~을 분해하다, 해체하다
2 delicious : =very pleasing, delightful
3 quaint creatures : 괴짜들
4 discoveries of hers : 그녀가 찾아낸 사람들
5 presentable : =looking good enough for people to see
6 a duck of a boy : 예쁜 아들 하나 *duck : 사랑스러운 사람, 귀여운 사람

adored her. They were rich, really rich, not just comfortably well off, which is odious and stuffy and sounds like one's grandparents. But if Rosemary wanted to shop she would go to Paris as you and I would go to Bond Street.[7] If she wanted to buy flowers, the car pulled up at that perfect shop in Regent Street, and Rosemary inside the shop just gazed in her dazzled, rather exotic way, and said: "I want those and those and those. Give me four bunches of those. And that jar of roses. Yes, I'll have all the roses in the jar. No, no lilac. I hate lilac. It's got no shape." The attendant[8] bowed and put the lilac out of sight, as though this was only too[9] true; lilac was dreadfully shapeless. "Give me those stumpy little tulips. Those red and white ones." And she was followed to the car by a thin shop-girl staggering under an immense white paper armful that looked like a baby in long clothes....

One winter afternoon she had been buying something in a little antique shop[10] in Curzon Street. It was a shop she liked.

7 Bond Street : 명품 브랜드 상점들이 줄지어 있는 런던의 고급 쇼핑가 ＊아래에 나오는 Regent Street도 마찬가지임.
8 the attendant : 종업원
9 only too : 매우, 아주, 무척
10 antique shop : 골동품 상점

For one thing, one usually had it to oneself.[11] And then the man who kept it was ridiculously fond of serving her. He beamed[12] whenever she came in. He clasped his hands; he was so gratified he could scarcely speak. Flattery, of course. All the same,[13] there was something....

"You see, madam," he would explain in his low respectful tones, "I love my things. I would rather not part with them than sell them to someone who does not appreciate them, who has not that fine feeling which is so rare...." And, breathing deeply, he unrolled a tiny square of blue velvet and pressed it on the glass counter with his pale finger-tips.

To-day it was a little box. He had been keeping it for her. He had shown it to nobody as yet. An exquisite little enamel box with a glaze[14] so fine it looked as though it had been baked in cream. On the lid a minute creature stood under a flowery tree, and a more minute creature still had her arms round his neck. Her hat, really no bigger than a geranium petal, hung from a branch; it had green ribbons. And there was a pink

---

11 one usually had it to oneself : (다른 손님 없이) 대개 혼자 차지했다

12 beam : 활짝 웃다

13 all the same : 그럼에도 불구하고

14 glaze : 광택, 윤

cloud like a watchful cherub[15] floating above their heads. Rosemary took her hands out of her long gloves. She always took off her gloves to examine such things. Yes, she liked it very much. She loved it; it was a great duck. She must have it. And, turning the creamy box, opening and shutting it, she couldn't help noticing how charming her hands were against the blue velvet. The shopman, in some dim cavern of his mind, may have dared to think so too. For he took a pencil, leant over the counter, and his pale, bloodless fingers crept timidly towards those rosy, flashing ones, as he murmured gently: "If I may venture to point out to madam, the flowers on the little lady's bodice."

"Charming!" Rosemary admired the flowers. But what was the price? For a moment the shopman did not seem to hear. Then a murmur reached her. "Twenty-eight guineas, madam."

"Twenty-eight guineas." Rosemary gave no sign. She laid the little box down; she buttoned her gloves again. Twenty-eight guineas. Even if one is rich.... She looked vague. She stared at a plump tea-kettle like a plump hen above the shopman's head,

---

15 cherub : 아기 천사, 천사 같은 아이

and her voice was dreamy as she answered: "Well, keep it for me — will you? I'll...."

But the shopman had already bowed as though keeping it for her was all any human being could ask. He would be willing, of course, to keep it for her for ever.

The discreet door shut with a click.[16] She was outside on the step, gazing at the winter afternoon. Rain was falling, and with the rain it seemed the dark came too, spinning down like ashes. There was a cold bitter taste in the air, and the new-lighted lamps looked sad. Sad were the lights in the houses opposite. Dimly they burned as if regretting something. And people hurried by, hidden under their hateful umbrellas. Rosemary felt a strange pang.[17] She pressed her muff against her breast; she wished she had the little box, too, to cling to. Of course the car was there. She'd only to cross the pavement. But still she waited. There are moments, horrible moments in life, when one emerges from shelter and looks out, and it's awful. One oughtn't to give way to them.[18] One ought to go

---

16 The discreet door shut with a click : 문은 딸깍 소리를 내며 조심스럽게 닫혔다

17 pang : 갑자기 격렬하게 일어나는 육체적(정신적) 고통

18 One oughtn't to give way to them : 그 끔찍한 순간에 무너져서는 안 된다

home and have an extra-special tea. But at the very instant of thinking that, a young girl, thin, dark, shadowy[19] — where had she come from? — was standing at Rosemary's elbow and a voice like a sigh, almost like a sob, breathed: "Madam, may I speak to you a moment?"

"Speak to me?" Rosemary turned. She saw a little battered creature with enormous eyes, someone quite young, no older than herself, who clutched[20] at her coat-collar with reddened hands, and shivered as though she had just come out of the water.

"M-madam," stammered the voice. "Would you let me have the price of a cup of tea?"

"A cup of tea?" There was something simple, sincere in that voice; it wasn't in the least the voice of a beggar. "Then have you no money at all?" asked Rosemary.

"None, madam," came the answer.

"How extraordinary!" Rosemary peered through the dusk and the girl gazed back at her. How more than extraordinary! And suddenly it seemed to Rosemary such an adventure. It was like something out of a novel by Dostoevsky, this meeting

---

19 shadowy : (어둑해서) 잘 보이지 않는, 어슴푸레한
20 clutch : 움켜잡다

in the dusk. Supposing she took the girl home? Supposing she did do one of those things she was always reading about or seeing on the stage, what would happen? It would be thrilling. And she heard herself saying afterwards to the amazement of her friends: "I simply took her home with me," as she stepped forward and said to that dim person beside her: "Come home to tea with me."

The girl drew back startled. She even stopped shivering for a moment. Rosemary put out a hand and touched her arm. "I mean it," she said, smiling. And she felt how simple and kind her smile was. "Why won't you? Do. Come home with me now in my car and have tea."

"You — you don't mean it, madam," said the girl, and there was pain in her voice.

"But I do," cried Rosemary. "I want you to. To please me. Come along."

The girl put her fingers to her lips and her eyes devoured[21] Rosemary. "You're — you're not taking me to the police station?" she stammered.

"The police station!" Rosemary laughed out.[22] "Why should

---

21 devour : 집어삼킬 듯이 바라보다, 뚫어지게 보다
22 laugh out : 웃음을 터뜨리다, 큰 소리로 웃다

I be so cruel? No, I only want to make you warm and to hear
— anything you care to tell me."

Hungry people are easily led.[23] The footman held the door
of the car open, and a moment later they were skimming[24]
through the dusk.

"There!" said Rosemary. She had a feeling of triumph as
she slipped her hand through the velvet strap. She could have
said, "Now I've got you," as she gazed at the little captive she
had netted. But of course she meant it kindly. Oh, more than
kindly. She was going to prove to this girl that — wonderful
things did happen in life, that — fairy godmothers[25] were real,
that — rich people had hearts, and that women were sisters.
She turned impulsively, saying, "Don't be frightened. After all,
why shouldn't you come back with me? We're both women. If
I'm the more fortunate, you ought to expect...."

But happily at that moment, for she didn't know how the
sentence was going to end, the car stopped. The bell was rung,
the door opened, and with a charming, protecting, almost
embracing movement, Rosemary drew the other into the

---

23 lead : (어떤 생각, 행동을) 하게 하다, 유인하다
24 skim : 스쳐 지나가다, 미끄러지듯 가다
25 fairy godmother : (어려울 때 나타나 도움을 주는 동화 속의) 요정대모

hall. Warmth, softness, light, a sweet scent, all those things so familiar to her she never even thought about them, she watched that other receive. It was fascinating. She was like the rich little girl in her nursery[26] with all the cupboards to open, all the boxes to unpack.

"Come, come upstairs," said Rosemary, longing to begin to be generous. "Come up to my room." And, besides, she wanted to spare this poor little thing from being stared at by the servants; she decided as they mounted the stairs she would not even ring to Jeanne,[27] but take off her things by herself. The great things were to be natural![28]

And "There!" cried Rosemary again, as they reached her beautiful big bedroom with the curtains drawn, the fire leaping on her wonderful lacquer furniture, her gold cushions and the primrose and blue rugs.

The girl stood just inside the door; she seemed dazed. But Rosemary didn't mind that.

"Come and sit down," she cried, dragging her big chair up to

---

26 nursery : (가정집의) 아기 방
27 Jeanne : 하녀의 이름으로 추정됨.
28 The great things were to be natural! : 훌륭한 일은 자연스러워야만 했다!

the fire, "in this comfy²⁹ chair. Come and get warm. You look so dreadfully cold."

"I daren't, madam," said the girl, and she edged³⁰ backwards.

"Oh, please," — Rosemary ran forward — "you mustn't be frightened, you mustn't, really. Sit down, when I've taken off 5 my things we shall go into the next room and have tea and be cozy. Why are you afraid?" And gently she half pushed the thin figure into its deep cradle.

But there was no answer. The girl stayed just as she had been put, with her hands by her sides and her mouth slightly open. 10 To be quite sincere, she looked rather stupid. But Rosemary wouldn't acknowledge it. She leant over her, saying: "Won't you take off your hat? Your pretty hair is all wet. And one is so much more comfortable without a hat, isn't one?"

There was a whisper that sounded like "Very good, madam," 15 and the crushed hat was taken off.

"And let me help you off with your coat, too," said Rose-mary.

The girl stood up. But she held on to³¹ the chair with one

---

29 comfy : <비격식> =comfortable
30 edge : 조금씩 움직이다
31 hold on to : ~에 매달리다, 붙잡다

hand and let Rosemary pull. It was quite an effort.[32] The other scarcely helped her at all. She seemed to stagger like a child, and the thought came and went through Rosemary's mind, that if people wanted helping they must respond a little, just a little, otherwise it became very difficult indeed. And what was she to do with the coat now? She left it on the floor, and the hat too. She was just going to take a cigarette off the mantelpiece when the girl said quickly, but so lightly and strangely: "I'm very sorry, madam, but I'm going to faint. I shall go off,[33] madam, if I don't have something."[34]

"Good heavens,[35] how thoughtless I am!" Rosemary rushed to the bell.

"Tea! Tea at once! And some brandy immediately!"

The maid was gone again, but the girl almost cried out: "No, I don't want no brandy. I never drink brandy. It's a cup of tea I want, madam." And she burst into tears.

It was a terrible and fascinating moment. Rosemary knelt beside her chair.

---

32 quite an effort : 꽤 힘든 일

33 go off : =faint, die

34 something : =something to eat

35 Good heavens! : 맙소사!, 큰일이군!, 저런!

"Don't cry, poor little thing," she said. "Don't cry." And she gave the other her lace handkerchief. She really was touched beyond words. She put her arm round those thin, bird-like shoulders.

Now at last the other forgot to be shy, forgot everything except that they were both women, and gasped out: "I can't go on no longer like this. I can't bear it. I can't bear it. I shall do away with myself. I can't bear no more."

"You shan't have to. I'll look after you. Don't cry any more. Don't you see what a good thing it was that you met me? We'll have tea and you'll tell me everything. And I shall arrange something. I promise. Do stop crying. It's so exhausting. Please!"

The other did stop just in time[36] for Rosemary to get up before the tea came. She had the table placed between them. She plied the poor little creature with everything,[37] all the sandwiches, all the bread and butter, and every time her cup was empty she filled it with tea, cream and sugar. People always said sugar was so nourishing. As for herself she didn't

---

36 just in time : 겨우 시간에 맞추어, 알맞은 때에

37 ply somebody with something : (특히 많은 음식 · 술을) ~에게 자꾸 주다 (권하다)

eat; she smoked and looked away tactfully so that the other should not be shy.

And really the effect of that slight meal was marvellous. When the tea-table was carried away a new being, a light, frail creature with tangled hair, dark lips, deep, lighted eyes, lay back in the big chair in a kind of sweet languor,[38] looking at the blaze. Rosemary lit a fresh cigarette; it was time to begin.

"And when did you have your last meal?" she asked softly.

But at that moment the door-handle turned.

"Rosemary, may I come in?" It was Philip.

"Of course."

He came in. "Oh, I'm so sorry," he said, and stopped and stared.

"It's quite all right," said Rosemary, smiling. "This is my friend, Miss — "

"Smith, madam," said the languid[39] figure, who was strangely still and unafraid.

"Smith," said Rosemary. "We are going to have a little talk."

"Oh yes," said Philip. "Quite," and his eye caught sight of the coat and hat on the floor. He came over to the fire and turned

---

38 sweet languor : 달콤한 나른함
39 languid : 힘없는, 활기 없는

his back to it. "It's a beastly[40] afternoon," he said curiously, still looking at that listless[41] figure, looking at its hands and boots, and then at Rosemary again.

"Yes, isn't it?" said Rosemary enthusiastically. "Vile."

Philip smiled his charming smile. "As a matter of fact," said he, "I wanted you to come into the library for a moment. Would you? Will Miss Smith excuse us?"

The big eyes were raised to him, but Rosemary answered for her: "Of course she will." And they went out of the room together.

"I say," said Philip, when they were alone. "Explain. Who is she? What does it all mean?"

Rosemary, laughing, leaned against the door and said: "I picked her up in Curzon Street. Really. She's a real pick-up. She asked me for the price of a cup of tea, and I brought her home with me."

"But what on earth are you going to do with her?" cried Philip.

"Be nice to her," said Rosemary quickly. "Be frightfully[42]

---

40 beastly: <비격식> =unpleasant, disagreeable
41 listless: 힘없는, 무기력한
42 frightfully: <비격식> =extremely

nice to her. Look after her. I don't know how. We haven't talked yet. But show her — treat her — make her feel — "

"My darling girl," said Philip, "you're quite mad, you know. It simply can't be done."

⁵ "I knew you'd say that," retorted Rosemary. "Why not? I want to. Isn't that a reason? And besides, one's always reading about these things. I decided — "

"But," said Philip slowly, and he cut the end of a cigar, "she's so astonishingly pretty."

¹⁰ "Pretty?" Rosemary was so surprised that she blushed. "Do you think so? I — I hadn't thought about it."

"Good Lord!"[43] Philip struck a match. "She's absolutely lovely. Look again, my child. I was bowled[44] over when I came into your room just now. However... I think you're making a ¹⁵ ghastly[45] mistake. Sorry, darling, if I'm crude and all that. But let me know if Miss Smith is going to dine with us in time for me to look up The Milliner's Gazette."

"You absurd creature!" said Rosemary, and she went out of the library, but not back to her bedroom. She went to her

---

43 Good Lord!: 맙소사! *놀람, 짜증, 걱정의 표현.

44 was bowled: 엄청나게 충격을 받았다

45 ghastly: =very bad, horrible

writing-room and sat down at her desk. Pretty! Absolutely lovely! Bowled over! Her heart beat like a heavy bell. Pretty! Lovely! She drew her check-book towards her. But no, checks would be no use, of course. She opened a drawer and took out five pound notes, looked at them, put two back, and holding the three squeezed in her hand, she went back to her bedroom.

Half an hour later Philip was still in the library, when Rosemary came in.

"I only wanted to tell you," said she, and she leaned against the door again and looked at him with her dazzled exotic gaze, "Miss Smith won't dine with us to-night."

Philip put down the paper. "Oh, what's happened? Previous engagement?"

Rosemary came over and sat down on his knee. "She insisted on going," said she, "so I gave the poor little thing a present of money. I couldn't keep her against her will, could I?" she added softly.

Rosemary had just done her hair, darkened her eyes a little, and put on her pearls. She put up her hands and touched Philip's cheeks.

"Do you like me?" said she, and her tone, sweet, husky, troubled him.

"I like you awfully," he said, and he held her tighter. "Kiss me."

There was a pause.

Then Rosemary said dreamily: "I saw a fascinating little box to-day. It cost twenty-eight guineas. May I have it?"

Philip jumped her on his knee. "You may, little wasteful one," said he.

But that was not really what Rosemary wanted to say.

"Philip," she whispered, and she pressed his head against her bosom, "am I pretty?"

작품 해설

1. 스냅 사진 한 장: "Am I pretty?"

  단편소설 특유의 '의외의 결말'(surprise ending)을 활용하고 있는 "A Cup of Tea"의 마지막 대목은 무척 당혹스런 결론이자 맥 빠진 반전이다. 특히 여성독자라면 더욱 불쾌할 수도 있는 결론으로, 굳이 페미니스트 운운하지 않더라도 누구나 종결부에서 표변(豹變)한 여주인공의 초라한 모습에 실망하지 않을 수 없기 때문이다. '차 한 잔'을 구걸하는 거지소녀를 만나 거창하게 시작한 주인공 Rosemary의 자선 프로젝트(?)는 갑자기 그녀의 질투심과 자격지심을 드러내는 우스꽝스런 해프닝으로 종결되고 만다. 사실 소녀를 집에 데려가 볼까 하는 생각은 그 나름의 의미 있는 결단이었다. 하지만 남편의 한마디가 문제였다. "그 아이가 엄청나게 이쁘더군."(she's so astonishingly pretty.) 아내가 데려온 거지소녀를 두고 남편이 툭 던진 한 마디 — 아내를 자극하기 위해 의도적으로 도발을 하였는지의 여부는 차치하고 — 는 그녀의 내면에 숨겨져 있던 예민하고 불안정한 지점을 정확하게 건드렸고, 그녀의 의식은 의욕적으로 시도하던 '세상 엿보기'를 중단하고 순식간에 자신/여성을 규정하는 남편의 시선으로 이동한다. 그 순간 Rosemary는 가난한 거지소녀를 돌보던 건강한 여성 주체에서 남편의 사랑을 갈구하는 나약하고 종속적인 대상으로 전락하고 마는 것이다. "A Cup of Tea"는 마치 한 인간/여성의 미묘하고 불안한 내면의 한 순간을 정직하게 포착해 낸 한 장의 스냅 사진에 가깝다.

2. 계급적 시각: 냉소와 풍자

Rosemary가 웬만큼 잘 사는 정도가 아니라 엄청난 상류층 인물이라는 점을 서술자가 언급하고 있다는 점을 감안한다면, 위에서 언급한 '미묘하고 불안한 내면 심리'의 문제를 인간/여성 일반의 문제라기보다 계급적 시각과 연관된 냉소와 풍자로 좁혀 보는 것도 가능해 보인다. "살다 보면 은신처에서 나와 바깥을 내다보는 순간들, 끔찍한 순간들이 있다."(There are moments, horrible moments in life, when one emerges from shelter and looks out.) 전지적 작가의 서술과 주인공의 내면 심리가 슬그머니 중첩되는 자유간접화법의 한 사례를 보여 주는 이 대목은 위에서 말한 대로 Rosemary의 기획에 나름의 진정성이 있음을 보여 준다. 그리고 마침내 그녀는 소녀를 집으로 데려오는 데 성공한다. 하지만 거기까지다. 상류층 귀부인 Rosemary의 자선 프로젝트는 즉흥성만큼이나 결함 많은 계획이며, 서술자는 최후의 파국이 오기 전 여러 단계마다 이 점을 놓치지 않고 암시한다. 그녀는 자신의 자선에 깜짝 놀라는 친구들의 모습을 기분 좋게 상상하거나 스스로를 동화 속의 요정대모(fairy godmother)로 그려 보는 허위의식도 감추지 못한다. 그것은 그녀의 자선이 상대에 대한 속 깊은 배려라는 자선의 기본을 망각한 자기중심적 과시에 불과하기 때문이다. 그렇기 때문에 그녀의 의식세계는 마치 친구를 불러 장난감이나 자랑하는 유치한 부잣집 딸 수

준에 머물러 있고, 굶주린 아이에게 엉뚱하게도 브랜디를 가져다주려는 황당한 실수를 저지르고 만다. '차 한 잔'을 청한 소녀 곁으로 다가가기에 Rosemary는 너무 높은 곳에 있었던 것이다.

3. 수미상관(首尾相關)

Rosemary의 몰락(?)이 충격적이긴 하나 모든 훌륭한 작품이 그렇듯이 작가는 미리 이 대반전의 근거를 예고해 두고 있었다는 점을 짚고 넘어갈 필요가 있다. 바로 작품의 첫 문장이다. "로즈메리 펠은 딱히 미인이라고 할 수는 없었다."(Rosemary Fell was not exactly beautiful.) 무심결에 읽게 되는 첫 문장은 작품 정독 후 다시 읽어 보면 마지막 문장 "나 예뻐요?"(Am I pretty?)와 수미상관에 가까운 정확한 대구를 이루기 때문이다. 남편의 무릎에서 어리광을 부리며 던지는 그녀의 질문에 대한 대답은 이미 첫 문장에 강력하게 주어져 있었던 셈이다. 이후의 이야기는 세상 밖으로 향하는 그녀의 모험이 얼마나 많은 한계를 지니고 있는지를 여실히 드러내며 최후의 반전을 향해 착실히 다가가고 있다.

영미 명작 단편선_3

The Sniper

Liam O'Flaherty

Liam O'Flaherty(1896~1984)는 20세기 초중반에 활동한 아일랜드 소설가이다. 아일랜드는 여전히 영국의 정치적 지배를 받는 상황이었지만, 19세기 후반부터 20세기 초반까지 자신들의 고유한 문학과 문화, 전통의 부흥을 꾀하는 Irish Renaissance(혹은 Celtic Revival)로 불리는 민족주의 성향의 문화운동이 전개되고 있었고 O'Flaherty도 그 활동가 중의 한 사람이었다. 사회주의자이자 공산주의자로서 반영 독립운동에도 가담했던 그는 작품 창작을 통해 자신의 신념을 실천에 옮긴 인물이다. "The Sniper"(1923)는 아일랜드 독립을 전후하여 복잡하게 전개된 아일랜드 내전(Irish Civil War)을 배경으로 전쟁의 비극, 몰인간성을 섬뜩하게 보여 주는 깔끔한 수작이다.

The Sniper

    The long June twilight faded into night. Dublin lay enveloped in darkness but for the dim light of the moon that shone through fleecy clouds, casting a pale light as of approaching dawn over the streets and the dark waters of the Liffey.[1] Around the beleaguered Four Courts[2] the heavy guns[3] roared. Here and there through the city, machine guns and rifles broke the silence of the night, spasmodically, like dogs barking on lone farms. Republicans and Free Staters[4] were waging civil war.

---

1 the Liffey: 리피강 ＊Dublin 시내를 서에서 동으로 가로질러 아일랜드해로 흐르는 강.
2 Four Courts: Ireland 대법원을 비롯한 주요 법원이 있는 Dublin 시내 중심부의 건물로 리피강 북쪽에 위치
3 the heavy guns: 중포(重砲)
4 Republicans and Free Staters: 공화국파와 자유국파 ＊전자는 아일랜드 전체의 완전한 독립을, 후자는 북아일랜드가 제외된 당시의 자유국 임시정부를 지지하였음.

On a rooftop near O'Connell Bridge, a Republican sniper lay watching. Beside him lay his rifle and over his shoulders was slung a pair of field glasses.[5] His face was the face of a student, thin and ascetic, but his eyes had the cold gleam of the fanatic. They were deep and thoughtful, the eyes of a man who is used to looking at death.

He was eating a sandwich hungrily. He had eaten nothing since morning. He had been too excited to eat. He finished the sandwich, and, taking a flask of whiskey from his pocket, he took a short drought.[6] Then he returned the flask to his pocket. He paused for a moment, considering whether he should risk a smoke. It was dangerous. The flash might be seen in the darkness, and there were enemies watching. He decided to take the risk.

Placing a cigarette between his lips, he struck a match, inhaled the smoke hurriedly and put out the light. Almost immediately, a bullet flattened[7] itself against the parapet of the roof. The sniper took another whiff[8] and put out the cigarette.

---

5 field glasses : 쌍안경
6 a short drought : <비격식> (위스키 같은 독한 술을 작은 잔으로) 한 잔
7 flatten : (건물, 나무 등을) 깨부수다, 넘어뜨리다
8 whiff : (잠깐 동안) 훅 끼치는(풍기는) 냄새

Then he swore softly and crawled away to the left.

Cautiously he raised himself and peered over the parapet. There was a flash and a bullet whizzed over his head. He dropped immediately. He had seen the flash. It came from the opposite side of the street.

He rolled over the roof to a chimney stack[9] in the rear, and slowly drew himself up behind it, until his eyes were level with the top of the parapet. There was nothing to be seen — just the dim outline of the opposite housetop against the blue sky. His enemy was under cover.

Just then an armored car[10] came across the bridge and advanced slowly up the street. It stopped on the opposite side of the street, fifty yards ahead. The sniper could hear the dull panting of the motor. His heart beat faster. It was an enemy car. He wanted to fire, but he knew it was useless. His bullets would never pierce the steel that covered the gray monster.

Then round the corner of a side street came an old woman, her head covered by a tattered[11] shawl. She began to talk to

---

9 a chimney stack: (공장 따위의) 높은 굴뚝

10 an armored car: 장갑차

11 tattered: 낡을 대로 낡은, 누더기가 된

the man in the turret[12] of the car. She was pointing to the roof where the sniper lay. An informer.[13]

The turret opened. A man's head and shoulders appeared, looking toward the sniper. The sniper raised his rifle and fired. The head fell heavily on the turret wall. The woman darted[14] toward the side street. The sniper fired again. The woman whirled round and fell with a shriek into the gutter.[15]

Suddenly from the opposite roof a shot rang out and the sniper dropped his rifle with a curse. The rifle clattered[16] to the roof. The sniper thought the noise would wake the dead. He stooped to pick the rifle up. He couldn't lift it. His forearm was dead.[17] "I'm hit," he muttered.

Dropping flat onto the roof, he crawled back to the parapet. With his left hand he felt the injured right forearm. The blood was oozing through the sleeve of his coat. There was no pain — just a deadened sensation, as if the arm had been cut off.

Quickly he drew his knife from his pocket, opened it on the

---

12 the turret : (전함, 탱크 등의) 회전 포탑
13 an informer : 밀고자, 정보제공자
14 dart : =run swiftly
15 the gutter : 길가의 하수도, 배수로
16 clatter : 달가닥 하는 소리를 내다
17 dead : 감각이 없는, 작동을 하지 않는

breastwork[18] of the parapet, and ripped open the sleeve. There was a small hole where the bullet had entered. On the other side there was no hole. The bullet had lodged[19] in the bone. It must have fractured it. He bent the arm below the wound. The arm bent back easily. He ground his teeth to overcome the pain.

Then taking out his field dressing,[20] he ripped open the packet[21] with his knife. He broke the neck of the iodine bottle and let the bitter fluid drip into the wound. A paroxysm of pain[22] swept through him. He placed the cotton wadding[23] over the wound and wrapped the dressing over it. He tied the ends with his teeth.

Then he lay still against the parapet, and, closing his eyes, he made an effort of will to overcome the pain.

In the street beneath all was still. The armored car had

---

18 on the breastwork: 흉장(흉벽)에 대고 *breastwork: 흉장, 흉벽. 적의 공격으로부터 아군을 보호하기 위해 가슴 높이로 쌓은 임시 구조물.

19 lodge: (총알 등이) 박히다, (화살 등이) 꽂히다

20 field dressing: 야전 붕대

21 packet: (종이 · 마분지로 된 상품 포장용) 통(갑)

22 a paroxysm of pain: 격렬한 통증

23 the cotton wadding: 솜 뭉텅이, 솜 마개

retired speedily over the bridge, with the machine gunner's[24] head hanging lifeless over the turret. The woman's corpse lay still in the gutter.

The sniper lay still for a long time nursing his wounded arm and planning escape. Morning must not find him wounded on the roof. The enemy on the opposite roof covered[25] his escape. He must kill that enemy and he could not use his rifle. He had only a revolver to do it. Then he thought of a plan.

Taking off his cap, he placed it over the muzzle of his rifle. Then he pushed the rifle slowly upward over the parapet, until the cap was visible from the opposite side of the street. Almost immediately there was a report,[26] and a bullet pierced the center of the cap. The sniper slanted the rifle forward. The cap clipped down into the street. Then catching the rifle in the middle, the sniper dropped his left hand over the roof and let it hang, lifelessly. After a few moments he let the rifle drop to the street. Then he sank to the roof, dragging his hand with him.

Crawling quickly to his feet, he peered up at the corner of

---

24 the machine gunner : 기관총 사수
25 cover : 총으로 봉쇄하다, 총을 겨누다
26 report : 총성, 포성, 폭발음

the roof. His ruse[27] had succeeded. The other sniper, seeing the cap and rifle fall, thought that he had killed his man. He was now standing before a row of chimney pots, looking across, with his head clearly silhouetted[28] against the western

5 sky.

The Republican sniper smiled and lifted his revolver above the edge of the parapet. The distance was about fifty yards — a hard shot in the dim light, and his right arm was paining him like a thousand devils.[29] He took a steady aim.[30] His hand

10 trembled with eagerness. Pressing his lips together, he took a deep breath through his nostrils and fired. He was almost deafened with the report and his arm shook with the recoil.[31]

Then when the smoke cleared, he peered across and uttered a cry of joy. His enemy had been hit. He was reeling over

15 the parapet in his death agony. He struggled to keep his feet, but he was slowly falling forward as if in a dream. The rifle fell from his grasp, hit the parapet, fell over, bounded off the

---

27 ruse : 책략, 계략

28 silhouette : 검은 윤곽을 드러내다

29 was paining him like a thousand devils : 엄청나게 아팠다

30 take a steady aim : 차분히 겨누다

31 recoil : (총포의) 반동, 뒤로 물러남

pole of a barber's shop beneath and then clattered on the pavement.

Then the dying man on the roof crumpled up[32] and fell forward. The body turned over and over in space and hit the ground with a dull thud. Then it lay still.

The sniper looked at his enemy falling and he shuddered. The lust of battle[33] died in him. He became bitten by remorse.[34] The sweat stood out in beads on his forehead. Weakened by his wound and the long summer day of fasting and watching on the roof, he revolted from[35] the sight of the shattered mass of his dead enemy. His teeth chattered, he began to gibber to himself, cursing the war, cursing himself, cursing everybody.

He looked at the smoking revolver in his hand, and with an oath[36] he hurled it to the roof at his feet. The revolver went off with a concussion[37] and the bullet whizzed past the sniper's head. He was frightened back to his senses by the shock. His

---

32 crumple up : (다치거나 술에 취해) 쓰러지다, 허물어지다
33 the lust of battle : 전투 본능, 전쟁욕
34 be bitten by remorse : 후회에 사로잡히다
35 revolt from : 비위에 거슬리다, 구역질 나다
36 with an oath : 욕설을 하며
37 go off with a concussion : 충격으로 발사되다

nerves steadied. The cloud of fear[38] scattered from his mind and he laughed.

Taking the whiskey flask from his pocket, he emptied it a drought. He felt reckless under the influence of the spirit.[39] He decided to leave the roof now and look for his company commander,[40] to report. Everywhere around was quiet. There was not much danger in going through the streets. He picked up his revolver and put it in his pocket. Then he crawled down through the skylight[41] to the house underneath.

When the sniper reached the laneway on the street level, he felt a sudden curiosity as to the identity of the enemy sniper whom he had killed. He decided that he was a good shot,[42] whoever he was. He wondered did he know him. Perhaps he had been in his own company before the split[43] in the army. He decided to risk going over to have a look at him. He peered around the corner into O'Connell Street. In the upper part of the street there was heavy firing, but around here all was quiet.

---

38 the cloud of fear : 공포의 먹구름
39 under the influence of the spirit : 술기운에
40 company commander : 중대장
41 skylight : (천장에 낸) 채광창
42 a good shot : 능숙한 사수
43 the split : 자유국파(Free Staters)와 공화국파(Republicans)의 분열

The sniper darted across the street. A machine gun tore up the ground around him with a hail of bullets,[44] but he escaped. He threw himself face downward beside the corpse. The machine gun stopped.

Then the sniper turned over the dead body and looked into 5 his brother's face.

44 a hail of bullets: 쏟아지는 총알

작품 해설

1. 슬픈 아일랜드

아일랜드 전문가인 역사학자 박지향 교수(서울대)는 아일랜드 역사와 문화, 문학을 다룬 책을 내며 제목을 '슬픈 아일랜드'라고 붙였다. 스스로를 세상에서 가장 슬픈 민족이라고 부르는 아일랜드인들의 정서 ─ 말하자면 아일랜드식 '한'(恨)의 정서 ─ 를 인상적으로 함축한 말이다. 이 슬픔의 배경에 이웃나라 영국이 있다. 한국과 일본 사이의 악연만큼이나 아일랜드와 영국 사이에 켜켜이 쌓인 역사적 앙금은 쉽게 지울 수 없는 상흔으로 남아 있기 때문이다. 한국인들이 겪은 임진왜란이나 일제강점기 35년의 치욕에 비해 아일랜드에 대한 영국의 직간접 지배는 시간적으로도 거의 700여년에 달하고, 그로 인한 상처의 폭과 깊이도 우리와는 비교할 수 없을 만큼 넓고 깊다. 한반도의 분리와 마찬가지로 1921년 독립 당시 북아일랜드(Northern Ireland)는 안타깝게도 독립국에 합류하지 못하고 영국(United Kingdom)의 일부로 잔류할 수밖에 없었고, 이후 100여년이 지난 지금도 아일랜드공화국과의 통합 가능성은 거의 없어 보인다.

더욱이 이들은 영토뿐만 아니라 자신들의 고유어마저 잃어버릴 처지가 되었다. 아일랜드 켈트족의 고유어인 게일어(Irish, Gaelic)가 공용어로 지정되어 있지만, 이제 극히 일부를 제외하고 주민들은 대부분 일상적으로 영어를 사용하고 있기 때문이다. 아일랜드 역사의 어두운 한 단면을 포착한 "The Sniper"가 게일어가 아닌 영어로 서술되었다는 아이러니가 '슬픈 아일랜드' 역사의 한 장을 보여 주는 셈이다. 지배자의 언어였던 영어가 아일랜드의 제1언어(the first language)가 됨으로써 역설적으로 국제사회에서 영어가 아일랜드 국가경쟁력의 원천으로 거론되고 있다는 씁쓸한 논리가 만들어지기도 한다. 그리고 무엇보다 우울한 사실은 영국의 오랜 지배 과정에서 발생한 민족 간의 통혼(intermarriage) 혹은 영국계 주민의 이주·정착 등으로 인해 아일랜드계 영국인, 영국계 아일랜드인이라고 하는 인종적 범주가 만들어졌고, 이로 인해 이제는 '누가 아일랜드인인가'(Who is Irish?)라는 곤혹스런 물음까지 가능해졌다는 점이다. 유감스럽게도 아일랜드인들의 민족적 정체성에 대한 혼란마저 발생한 것이다.

2. 내전/전쟁의 비극

"그리고 저격수는 죽은 이의 몸을 뒤집어 그의 형의 얼굴을 들여다보았다."(Then the sniper turned over the dead body and looked into his brother's face.) 사실 위주의 묘사로 무미건조하게 서술하고 있지만, 작품의 마지막 장면은 사실 충격적인 진실을 전하고 있다. 저격수가 사살한 적군은 놀랍게도 바로 자신의 형(혹은 동생)이었던 것이다. 아일랜드 내전 당시 공화국파(Republicans) 청년 병사를 주인공으로 설정한 "The Sniper"는 전쟁이 형제와 동료를 죽이는 야만적 행위라는 사실을 그 어떤 논리보다 더 리얼하게 전하고 있다. 공화국파는 영국 정부와의 타

협을 거부한 이들로, 장차 아일랜드공화군(IRA)으로 발전하는 과격파라는 점에서 청년병사의 전투 본능(the lust of battle)은 더욱 더 설득력을 지닌다. 그렇기 때문에 학업을 잠시 중단하고 전쟁판에 끼어든 청년의 깡마른 얼굴에는 금욕주의자의 면모가 있었고, 죽음에 익숙한 그의 두 눈에는 광기가 서려 있었던 것이다. 전쟁은 승리가 목적이지만 이렇게 되면 최종적으로 전쟁은 승자가 없는 싸움이 되고 만다. 그가 사살한 형(혹은 동생)은 말할 것도 없고 기관총 사수나 밀고자 노파 모두 그의 형제라는 사실을 작품의 마지막 문장은 강력하게 암시하고 있기 때문이다.

요컨대 제국주의와 식민지 지배가 피지배자들 간의 갈등과 반목, 분열을 초래하고 또 이용한다는 점은 새삼스러울 것도 없는 이야기가 되었지만, 아일랜드 내전을 소재로 한 단편 "The Sniper"는 이러한 갈등과 분열을 가장 생생하게 또 가장 비극적으로 재현하는 데 성공하였으며, 역사를 넘어 전쟁 그 자체의 아이러니한 비극성을 생생하게 증언하고 있다.

3. 문체의 역할: concise and hardboiled

이 작품이 내전/전쟁의 비극성을 충격적으로 전달하는 데는 '간결하고 무미건조한'(concise and hardboiled) 문체도 한몫을 한다. 6월 어느 날 저녁 무렵 Dublin 거리의 풍경 묘사에서 시작한 서술은 최소한의 단어로 이루어진 인물의 외관과 행동 묘사로 이어지고 있고, 이렇게 구축된 건조한 분위기는 전쟁과 전투의 몰인간성, 비인간성을 드러내는 데 일조하고 있다. 단문을 활용한 간결체는 빠른 사건 전개로 극적 긴장감을 창출해 내고 있고, 감정묘사를 절제한 건조체는 심리묘사 없이도 전쟁으로 경화된 주인공의 내면을 충분히 전달할 수 있음을 보여 준다. 이를테면 옥상 위의 청년 저격수는 광신에 가까운 확신을 가지고 전투에 참여하고 있고, 적을 조준 사격하는 그의 전투 본능은 거의 전쟁 기계라고 할 만큼 정밀하게 수행되고 있으며, 추락한 적 저격수의 신원을 확인하는 그의 호기심은 다시 그가 동정과 공감을 지닌 인간으로 돌아와 있음을 알려 준다. 하지만 이 모든 내면 변화의 어느 대목에서도 서술자는 주인공의 내면으로 들어가는 모험을 하지 않는다. 담담하게 감정을 억제하며 사실만을 묘사할 뿐이다. 마지막 장면에 맞닥뜨리는 '진실의 순간'(a moment of truth)이 더욱 충격적인 것은 이와 같이 건조한 문체를 통해 탄탄하게 구축된 정조가 있기 때문이다.

영미 명작 단편선_4

The Story of the Siren

E. M. Forster

E. M. Forster(1879~1970)는 20세기 초반의 영국 소설가로, 대표작으로는 *Howards End*(1910)와 *A Passage to India*(1924) 등이 있다. 두 작품 모두 작가가 가정 내부 또는 국가 간의 대립적인 문화와 양식 사이에서 벌어지는 갈등과 충돌에 관심이 있음을 잘 보여 준다. 빅토리아 시대 특유의 체면과 속박, 규범을 벗어나 좀 더 자유주의적이고 진보적인 사상과 경향에 우호적이었던 그는, 지중해적 이교주의(paganism)로 지칭할 만한 남유럽적—특히 이탈리아와 그리스를 배경으로 한—원초적 정서와 신비주의에 대한 호감을 여러 단편에서 드러내는데, "The Story of the Siren"(1920)도 그 범주에 속한다. 전설 속 사이렌(Siren)의 신화를 사실(fact)로 받아들이는 원주민 여행 가이드의 이야기를 통해 서술자가 신비의 세계에 조금씩 공감하는 모습이 흥미롭게 전개된다.

The Story of the Siren

Few things have been more beautiful than my note book on the Deist Controversy[1] as it fell downward through the waters of the Mediterranean. It dived, like a piece of black slate,[2] but opened soon, disclosing leaves of pale green, which quivered into blue. Now it had vanished, now it was a piece of magical india rubber[3] stretching out to infinity, now it was a book again, but bigger than the book of all knowledge.[4] It grew more fantastic as it reached the bottom, where a puff of sand welcomed it[5] and obscured it from view. But it reappeared,

---

1 the Deist Controversy : 이신론(理神論, Deism) 논쟁 ＊계시나 기적 등을 부정하고 성서를 비판적으로 연구할 것을 주장하는 합리주의적 기독교 신학이론을 가리킴.
2 black slate : 흑색 점판암
3 india rubber : 지우개 고무
4 the book of all knowledge : 백과사전류의 당시 서적으로 추정됨.
5 a puff of sand welcomed it : 모래가 풀썩 일어나 공책을 반겼다

quite sane though a little tremulous,[6] lying decently open on its back, while unseen fingers[7] fidgeted among its leaves.

"It is such a pity," said my aunt, "that you will not finish your work in the Hotel. Then you would be free to enjoy yourself and this would never have happened."

"Nothing of it but will change into something rich and strange,"[8] warbled the chaplain, while his sister said "Why, it's gone into the water." As for the boatmen, one of them laughed, while the other, without a word of warning, stood up and began to take his clothes off.

"Holy Moses!"[9] cried the Colonel. "Is the fellow mad?"

"Yes, thank him dear," said my aunt: "that is to say tell him he is very kind, but perhaps another time."[10]

"All the same[11] I do want my book back," I complained. "It's

---

6 quite sane though a little tremulous: 약간 불안하지만 차분한 상태로

7 unseen fingers: 바닷속의 물결을 뜻함.

8 Nothing of it but will change into something rich and strange: 그것이 뭔가 풍요롭고 진기한 것으로 변하지 않는 것은 아니지 *공책이 물속에서 썩을 것을 반어적으로 표현한 말로, 'Not but that ~' 구문의 변형으로 볼 수 있음.

9 Holy Moses!: 이런!

10 perhaps another time: (지금은 말고) 이 다음에 *정중한 사양을 나타낼 때 사용함.

11 all the same: =nevertheless

for my Fellowship Dissertation.[12] There won't be much left of it by another time."

"I have an idea," said some woman or other through her parasol. "Let us leave this child of nature to dive for the book
5 while we go on to the other grotto.[13] We can land him either on this rock or on the ledge[14] inside, and he will be ready when we return."

The idea seemed good; and I improved it by saying I would be left behind too, to lighten the boat. So the two of us were
10 deposited outside the little grotto on a great sunlit rock that guarded the harmonies within. Let us call them blue, though they suggest rather the spirit of what is clean — cleanliness passed from the domestic to the sublime,[15] the cleanliness of all the sea gathered together and radiating light. The Blue
15 Grotto at Capri[16] contains only more blue water, not bluer

---

12 Fellowship Dissertation : 펠로우십 논문 ＊영국 대학에서 펠로우는 교수 아래 전임강사급의 교육 및 연구 직급을 가리킴.

13 grotto : 작은 동굴

14 ledge : 바위 턱, 돌출부

15 cleanliness passed from the domestic to the sublime : 가정적인 정결함을 넘어 숭고의 차원으로 올라선 정결함

16 The Blue Grotto at Capri : 카프리섬의 (유명한 관광지인) 푸른 동굴(해식 동) ＊Blue Grotto는 이탈리아어로 Grotta Azzurra라고 함.

water. That colour and that spirit is the heritage[17] of every cave in the Mediterranean into which the sun can shine and the sea flow.

As soon as the boat left I realized how imprudent I had been to trust myself on a sloping rock with an unknown Sicilian. With a jerk[18] he became alive, seizing my arm and saying, "Go to the end of the grotto and I will show you something beautiful."

He made me jump off the rock on to the ledge over a dazzling crack of sea; he drew me away from the light till I was standing on the tiny beach of sand which emerged like powdered turquoise[19] at the further end. There he left me with his clothes, and returned swiftly to the summit of the entrance rock. For a moment he stood naked in the brilliant sun, looking down at the spot where the book lay. Then he crossed himself,[20] raised his hands above his head, and dived.

If the book was wonderful, the man is past all description.[21]

---

17 the heritage : 여기서는 '변함없는 특성'이란 뜻.
18 with a jerk : 갑자기, 홱
19 powdered turquoise : 터키석 가루
20 cross oneself : 성호를 긋다
21 past all description : 말로 다할 수 없을 만큼

His effect[22] was that of a silver statue, alive beneath the sea, through whom life throbbed in blue and green. Something infinitely happy, infinitely wise — but it was impossible that it should emerge from the depths[23] sunburnt and dripping, holding the note book on the Deist Controversy between its teeth.

A gratuity is generally expected by those who bathe. Whatever I offered, he was sure to want more, and I was disinclined for an argument in a place so beautiful and also so solitary. It was a relief that he should say in conversational tones,[24] "In a place like this one might see the Siren."

I was delighted with him for thus falling into the key[25] of his surroundings. We had been left together in a magic world, apart from all the commonplaces that are called reality, a world of blue whose floor was the sea and whose walls and roof of rock trembled with the sea's reflections. Here, only the fantastic would be tolerable, and it was in that spirit that I echoed his words, "One might easily see the Siren."

---

22 effect : (화가 · 작가 등이 만들어 내는) 느낌(인상)
23 the depths : 깊은 바닷속
24 in conversational tones : 스스럼없는 말투로
25 key : 분위기, 풍조, 경향

He watched me curiously while he dressed. I was parting[26] the sticky leaves of the note book as I sat on the sand.

"Ah," he said at last. "You may have read the little book that was printed last year. Who would have thought that our Siren would have given the foreigners pleasure!"

5

(I read it afterwards. Its account[27] is, not unnaturally,[28] incomplete, in spite of there being a woodcut[29] of the young person, and the words of her song.)

"She comes out of this blue water, doesn't she," I suggested, "and sits on the rock at the entrance, combing her hair."

10

I wanted to draw him out,[30] for I was interested in his sudden gravity,[31] and there was a suggestion of irony[32] in his last remark that puzzled me.

"Have you ever seen her?"

"Often and often."

15

"I, never."

---

26 part: 떼어 내다

27 account: (있었던 일에 대한) 설명, 이야기

28 not unnaturally: 당연한 일이지만

29 woodcut: 목판화

30 draw him out: 그의 이야기를 끌어내다

31 gravity: 진지함, 엄숙함

32 a suggestion of irony: 빈정거리는 기미

"But you have heard her sing!"

He put on his coat and said impatiently, "How can she sing under the water? Who could? She sometimes tries, but nothing comes from her but great bubbles."

"She should climb on to the rock."

"How can she?" he cried again, quite angry. "The priests have blessed[33] the air, so she cannot breathe it, and blessed the rocks, so that she cannot sit on them. But the sea no man can bless, because it is too big, and always changing. Therefore she lives in the sea."

I was silent.

At this[34] his face took a gentler expression. He looked at me as though something was on his mind,[35] and going out to the entrance rock gazed at the external blue. Then returning into our twilight he said, "As a rule only good people see the Siren."

I made no comment. There was a pause, and he continued. "That is a very strange thing, and the priests do not know how to account for it; for she of course is wicked. Not only those

---

33 bless: 축성(祝聖)하다
34 At this: 이 말을 하고
35 as though something was on his mind: 뭔가 마음에 걸리는 듯

who fast and go to mass are in danger,[36] but even those who are merely good in daily life. No one in the village had seen her for two generations. I am not surprised. We all cross ourselves before we enter the water, but it is unnecessary. Giuseppe, we thought, was safer than most.[37] We loved him, and many of us he loved: but that is a different thing from being good."

I asked who Giuseppe was.

"That day — I was seventeen and my brother was twenty and a great deal stronger than I was and it was the year when the visitors, who have brought such prosperity and so many alterations into the village, first began to come. One English lady in particular, of very high birth,[38] came, and has written a book about the place, and it was through her that the Improvement Syndicate[39] was formed, which is about to connect the hotels with the station by means of a funicular railway."[40]

"Don't tell me about that lady in here," I observed.

---

36 in danger : =in danger of meeting the Siren
37 safer than most : 누구보다도 안전한
38 of very high birth : 매우 지체가 높은
39 the Improvement Syndicate : 지역 개발 조합
40 a funicular railway : =a cable railway. 케이블카

"That day we took her and her friends to see the grottoes. As we rowed close under the cliffs I put out my hand, as one does,[41] and caught a little crab, and having pulled off its claws offered it as a curiosity.[42] The ladies groaned, but a gentleman was pleased, and held out money. Being inexperienced, I refused it, saying that his pleasure was sufficient reward! Giuseppe, who was rowing behind, was very angry with me and reached out with his hand and hit me on the side of the mouth, so that a tooth cut my lip, and I bled. I tried to hit him back, but he always was too quick for me, and as I stretched round he kicked me under the arm pit,[43] so that for a moment I could not even row. There was a great noise among the ladies, and I heard afterwards that they were planning to take me away from my brother and train me as a waiter. That at all events never came to pass.[44]

"When we reached the grotto — not here, but a larger one — the gentleman was very anxious that one of us should dive for money, and the ladies consented, as they sometimes do.

---

41   as one does : 흔히 그렇듯이

42   curiosity : 진기한 것

43   arm pit : 겨드랑이

44   come to pass : =happen

Giuseppe who had discovered how much pleasure it gives foreigners to see us in the water, refused to dive for anything but silver,[45] and the gentleman threw in a two lira piece.

"Just before my brother sprang off he caught sight of me holding my bruise, and crying, for I could not help it. He laughed and said, 'this time, at all events, I shall not see the Siren!' and went into the blue water without crossing himself. But he saw her."

He broke off, and accepted a cigarette. I watched the golden entrance rock and the quivering walls, and the magic water through which great bubbles constantly rose.

At last he dropped his hot ash into the ripples and turned his head away, and said, "He came up without the coin. We pulled him into the boat, and he was so large that he seemed to fill it, and so wet that we could not dress him. I have never seen a man so wet. I and the gentleman rowed back, and we covered Giuseppe with sacking[46] and propped him up[47] in the stern."

"He was drowned, then?" I murmured, supposing that to be

---

45 refused to dive for anything but silver : 은화가 아니면 절대로 잠수를 하지 않겠다고 했다

46 sacking : =sackcloth. 부대 만드는 천, 거친 삼베

47 prop somebody up : ~를 떠받치다, 지탱하다

the point.

"He was not," he cried angrily. "He saw the Siren. I told you."

I was silenced again.

"We put him to bed, though he was not ill. The doctor came,
and took money, and the priest came and took more and
smothered[48] him with incense and spattered him with holy
water.[49] But it was no good. He was too big — like a piece of
the sea. He kissed the thumb-bones of San Biagio[50] and they
never dried till evening."

"What did he look like?" I ventured.[51]

"Like anyone who has seen the Siren. If you have seen
her 'often and often' how is it you do not know? Unhappy,
unhappy, unhappy because he knew everything. Every living
thing made him unhappy because he knew it would die. And
all he cared to do was to sleep."

I bent over my note book.

"He did no work, he forgot to eat, he forgot whether he had

---

48 smother : 숨 막히게 하다
49 holy water : 성수, 사제가 축성한 물
50 San Biagio : 산 비아지오 조각상 *4세기경 이탈리아의 성자였던 산 비아지
     오는 질식이나 각종 목 관련 질환을 치료하는 데 영험하다는 속설이 있었음.
51 venture : 과감히 말하다

his clothes on. All the work fell on me, and my sister had to go out to service.[52] We tried to make him into a beggar, but he was too robust to inspire pity, and as for an idiot, he had not the right look[53] in his eyes. He would stand in the street looking at people, and the more he looked at them the more unhappy he became. When a child was born he would cover his face with his hands. If anyone was married — he was terrible then, and would frighten them as they came out of church. Who would have believed he would marry himself! I caused that, I. I was reading out of the paper how a girl at Ragusa[54] had 'gone mad through bathing in the sea.' Giuseppe got up, and in a week he and that girl came in together.

"He never told me anything, but it seems that he went straight to her house, broke into[55] her room, and carried her off. She was the daughter of a rich mineowner, so you may imagine our peril. Her father came down, with a clever lawyer, but they could do no more than I.[56] They argued and they

---

52 go out to service : 고용살이를 하러 가다
53 the right look : 딱 맞는(어울리는) 표정
54 Ragusa : 시칠리아섬 남부에 있는 도시
55 break into : 침입하다, 억지로 열다
56 they could do no more than I : 그들도 나와 마찬가지로 어쩔 수 없었다

threatened, but at last they had to go back and we lost nothing
— that is to say, no money. We took Giuseppe and Maria to
the Church and had them married. Ugh![57] that wedding! The
priest made no jokes[58] afterwards and coming out the children
threw stones.... I think I would have died to make her happy;
but as always happens, one could do nothing."

"Were they unhappy together then?"

"They loved each other, but love is not happiness. We can all
get love. Love is nothing. Love is everywhere since the death
of Jesus Christ. I had two people to work for[59] now, for she
was like him in everything — one never knew which of them
was speaking. I had to sell our own boat and work under the
bad old man you have[60] to-day. Worst of all, people began to
hate us. The children first — everything begins with them —
and then the women and last of all the men. For the cause of
every misfortune was — You will not betray me?"

I promised good faith,[61] and immediately he burst into the

---

57 Ugh!: 욱, 웩 *역겨움, 불쾌감을 나타내는 소리.

58 made no jokes: (결혼식 후에 으레 하는) 농담도 하지 않았다

59 work for: =support. 부양하다

60 have: 고용해 두고 있다

61 promise good faith: 비밀을 지키겠다고 약속하다

frantic blasphemy[62] of one who has escaped from supervision, cursing the priests, the lying filthy cheating immoral priests who had ruined his life, he said. "Thus are we tricked!" was his cry and he stood up and kicked at the azure ripples with his feet, till he had obscured them with a cloud of sand.

I too was moved. The story of Giuseppe, for all its absurdity and superstition,[63] came nearer to reality than anything I had known before. I don't know why, but it filled me with desire to help others — the greatest of all our desires, I suppose, and the most fruitless. The desire soon passed.

"She was about to have a child.[64] That was the end of everything. People said to me, 'When will your charming nephew be born? What a cheerful attractive child he will be, with such a father and mother!' I kept my face steady[65] and replied, 'I think he may be. Out of sadness shall come gladness' — it is one of our proverbs. And my answer frightened them very much, and they told the priests, who were frightened too.

---

62 burst into the frantic blasphemy : 엄청난 신성모독에 가까운 욕설을 터뜨리다

63 for all its absurdity and superstition : 그 터무니없고 미신 같은 내용에도 불구하고

64 have a child : 아기를 낳다

65 keep my face steady : 정색하다

Then the whisper started that the child would be Antichrist.[66] You need not be afraid: he was never born.

"An old witch began to prophesy, and no one stopped her. Giuseppe and the girl, she said, had silent devils, who could do little harm. But the child would always be speaking and laughing and perverting,[67] and last of all he would go into the sea and fetch up the Siren into the air and all the world would see her and hear her sing. As soon as she sang, the Seven Vials[68] would be opened and the Pope would die and Mongibello[69] flame, and the veil of Santa Agata[70] would be burnt. Then the boy and the Siren would marry, and together they would rule the world, for ever and ever.

"The whole village was in tumult, and the hotel keepers became alarmed, for the tourist season was just beginning.

---

66 Antichrist: 적그리스도 * 세상의 종말에 나타나 재림하는 그리스도와 대적할 것으로 예언된 통치자 혹은 영.

67 pervert: 나쁜 길로 들어서게 하다, 사람을 비뚤어지게 하다, 배교자가 되다

68 the Seven Vials: 신의 분노를 담은 일곱 개의 병 * 신약성서 Revelation 16 장 참조.

69 Mongibello: 몬지벨로 * 시칠리아섬 동부의 활화산인 에트나(Etna) 화산을 현지에서 부르는 이름.

70 the veil of Santa Agata: 성녀 아가타의 베일 * 이 지방 사람들이 신성하게 여기는 유물.

They met together and decided that Giuseppe and the girl must be sent inland until the child was born, and they subscribed the money. The night before they were to start there was a full moon and wind from the east, and all along the coast the sea shot up over the cliffs in silver clouds.[71] It is a wonderful sight, and Maria said she must see it once more.

"'Do not go,' I said. 'I saw the priest go by, and someone with him. And the hotel keepers do not like you to be seen, and if we displease them also we shall starve.'

"'I want to go,' she replied. 'The sea is stormy, and I may never feel it again.'

"'No, he is right,' said Giuseppe. 'Do not go — or let one of us go with you.'

"'I want to go alone.' she said; and she went alone.

"I tied up[72] their luggage in a piece of cloth, and then I was so unhappy at thinking I should lose them that I went and sat down by my brother and put my arm round his neck, and he put his arm round me, which he had not done for more than a year, and we remained thus I don't remember how long.

---

71 the sea shot up over the cliffs in silver clouds : 바닷물이 절벽에 부딪혀 은빛 구름으로 솟아올랐다

72 tied up : 단단히 묶었다

"Suddenly the door flew open[73] and moonlight and wind came in together, and a child's voice said laughing, 'They have pushed her over the cliffs into the sea.'

"I stepped to the drawer where I keep my knives.

"'Sit down again,' said Giuseppe — Giuseppe of all people![74] 'If she is dead, why should others die too?'"

"'I guess who it is,' I cried, 'and I will kill him.'"

"I was almost out of the door but he tripped me up[75] and kneeling upon me took hold of both my hands and sprained my wrists; first my right one, then my left. No one but Giuseppe would have thought of such a thing. It hurt more than you would suppose, and I fainted. When I woke up, he was gone, and I have never seen him again."

But Giuseppe disgusted me.[76]

"I told you he was wicked," he said. "No one would have expected him to see the Siren."

"How do you know he did see her?"

---

73 fly open : (문이) 휙 열리다
74 Giuseppe of all people! : 다른 사람이 아닌 바로 주세페가! *가장 격분해야 할 주세페가 오히려 자신을 말렸다는 뜻임.
75 tripped me up : 내 발을 걸었다
76 Giuseppe disgusted me : 나는 주세페가 혐오스러웠다

"Because he did not see her 'often and often' but once."

"Why do you love him if he is wicked?"

He laughed for the first time. That was his only reply.

"Is that the end?" I asked.

"I never killed her murderer, for by the time my wrists were well, he was in America; and one cannot kill a priest. As for Giuseppe, he went all over the world too, looking for someone else who has seen the Siren — either a man, or, better still, a woman, for then the child might still have been born. At last he came to Liverpool — is the district probable? — and there he began to cough, and spat blood until he died.

"I do not suppose there is anyone living now who has seen her. There has seldom been more than one in a generation, and never in my life will there be both a man and a woman from whom that child can be born, who will fetch up the Siren from the sea, and destroy silence, and save the world!"

"Save the world?" I cried. "Did the prophecy end like that?"

He leant back against the rock, breathing deep. Through all the blue-green reflections I saw him colour.[77] I heard him say: "Silence and loneliness cannot last for ever. It may be a

---

77 colour : 얼굴을 붉히다

hundred or a thousand years, but the sea lasts longer, and she shall come out of it and sing." I would have asked him more, but at that moment the whole cave darkened, and there rode in through its narrow entrance the returning boat.[78]

---

78 there rode in through its narrow entrance the returning boat : 좁은 입구를 통해 유람선이 돌아오고 있었다

작품 해설

⚘

1. the Mediterranean paganism

E. M. Forster의 소설에는 지중해 북부 이탈리아와 그리스 지역, 그리고 그곳 사람들과 그들의 문화, 전통에 대한 우호적 관심이 담겨 있는데, 어떤 평자는 이를 '지중해적 이교주의'(the Mediterranean paganism)라는 말로 표현했다. 로마제국의 국교로 인정받은 기독교 측에서는 그리스 · 로마 문명을 비롯한 기타 종교, 문명에 대해 이교도(pagan) 혹은 이교주의(paganism)라는 경멸적 용어를 사용하기 시작하는데, 유일신 신앙에 바탕을 둔 그들의 입장에서는 당연한 귀결이었다. 이에 따라 서양의 문화, 예술에서는 전통적으로 기독교 이외의 신앙, 종교와 관련된 것들에 이교적이란 이름표를 붙여 왔고, 서양 문명의 또 하나의 기둥에 해당하는 그리스 · 로마의 헬레니즘 문화까지도 이교적 전통(pagan tradition)이라는 분류를 피할 수 없었다.

역사적으로 서양 문명과 그 뿌리를 이루는 기독교에 대해 서구사회 내부의 자성이 일면서 그리스 · 로마 문화와 전승, 전통에 대한 관심이 증대되는 것은 자연스러운 귀결이었다. 위에서 지중해적 이교주의로 명명한 포스터의 호감 또한 19세기 말 이후 전개되는 진보적 반기독교 흐름을 일정 부분 반영한다. 특히 Forster는 20세 전후인 1900년대 초

실제로 그리스와 이탈리아 등을 여행하면서 남유럽의 풍광과 정서에 매료되었고, 이를 통해 그들의 삶과 문화, 정서에 대한 호감 또한 자연스럽게 생성되면서 이를 자신의 작품 배경과 소재로 활용하였다. 예로부터 혹독한 날씨의 영국이나 북유럽에서는 기후가 온화한 지중해 연안의 휴양지로 여행을 떠나는 것이 식자층이나 귀족 가문에서 누릴 수 있는 호사 중의 하나였고, 많은 문인, 예술가들이 남유럽 여행을 소재로 한 작품이나 기록을 남긴 것을 볼 수 있다.

2. 이원적 대립구도

그런 점에서 이 작품의 기본 플롯은 거의 도식적이라고 할 만큼 뚜렷한 이원적 대립구도로 설정되어 있다. "자연의 아이"(child of nature)로 불리는 시칠리아 원주민 여행 가이드는 전설 속 사이렌(Siren)의 존재를 굳게 믿고 있는 반면에, 그 이야기를 전해 듣는 영국인 서술자는 이신론(Deism), 곧 합리주의적 관점에서 종교를 연구하는 인물이다. 무엇보다도 지중해 푸른 바닷속으로 뛰어드는 가이드의 아름다운 육체를 "한없이 행복하고 한없이 지혜로운 무엇"(Something infinitely happy, infinitely wise)으로 묘사하는 대목에서부터 작가가 이 두 개의 대립항 중에서 어느 쪽 손을 들어 주는지 금방 알 수 있다. 사이렌을 목격한 Giuseppe가 진리를 일별한 인물로 설정되고, 최종적으로 원수를 용서하고 사랑하라는 기독교의 가르침을 실천하는 인물도 바로 세상에서 광인으로 부르는 Giuseppe였다는 점도 모두 같은 맥락에 있다.

그 밖의 다른 이원적 대립항들 역시 동일한 구도 속에 전개되고 있다. 신화 속의 존재 사이렌과 제도종교를 대표하는 기독교 사제, 사이렌의 노래와 육지의 침묵, 시칠리아의 아름다운 원주민과 경박스런 영국 관광객들, 늘 변화하며 살아 있는 거대한 바다와 신부의 축성으로 굳어 버린 육지 등이 이 대립구도의 다양한 양상이다. 그리고 이 모든 이야기를 호기심 어린 눈으로 바라보는 서술자는 지중해적 이교주의라고 함직한 관심을 통해 자신들의 세계 곧 영국, 영국인들의 삶과 문화를 돌아보고 있다.

3. 액자소설: 두 명의 화자

이 작품의 1차 화자는 이신론을 공부하는 청년으로, 작품 내용은 대부분 그가 시칠리아에서 만난 여행 가이드, 곧 2차 화자의 서술로 전개된다. 이야기 속에 이야기가 있는 이른바 액자소설(the frame story)이다. 작가들은 액자소설의 틀을 다양한 방식으로 활용하는데, 이 작품에서는 무엇보다도 현지인 가이드의 신비한 이야기에 신빙성을 부여하는 장치로 활용된다.

가이드의 이야기 자체는 사실 황당하기 짝이 없다. 성호를 긋지 않고 바닷속으로 들어간 탓에 형 Giuseppe는 전설 속의 사이렌을 보고 만다. 이를 통해 진리를 깨친 그는 자기와 같이 사이렌을 만난 여인과 결혼하지만 그녀는 결국 사제에게 살해당하고 말았고, 가이드는 혹시 형이 그런 여인을 다시 만날 수 있다면 그들에게서 태어난 아이가 마침내 바다에서 사이렌을 건져 내어 세상을 구원할 것이라고 전한다. 황당무계한 이야기지만, 그의 이야기를 진지하게 경청하는 화자의 존재로 인해 Giuseppe와 사이렌의 이야기는 신비로운 진리에 가까운 무게감을 지니게 된다. 그리고 Giuseppe의 이야기를 통해 1차 화자는 마치 진리를 일별한 듯한 순간적인 깨달음을 얻게 되는데, 이는 애당초 그가 다른 경박한 관광객들과 구별되는 인물로 설정되어 있기 때문에 더욱 신빙성을 지니게 된다. 작품의 마지막 장면은 그가 목격한 새로운 세계의 의미에 대해 복합적인 함의를 더한다. "나는 그에게 더 묻고 싶었지만, 그 순간 동굴 전체가 어두워지면서 좁은 입구를 통해 유람선이 돌아오고 있었다."(I would have asked him more, but at that moment the whole cave darkened, and there rode in through its narrow entrance the returning boat.) 마치 마법의 세계에 빠져들 듯 그는 지금까지 가이드의 이야기에 귀를 기울이고 있었지만 동굴로 돌아오는 유람선은 그를 다시 현실의 세계로 끌어내기 때문이다. 유람선과 그 배를 탄 관광객들을 통해 강력한 현실 환기가 이루어지면서 사이렌의 신비한 이야기는 더욱 뚜렷한 대조 효과를 얻는 것이다.

영미 명작 단편선_5

Half-Holiday

Aldous Huxley

Aldous Huxley(1894~1963)는 일반 대중에게는 1932년에 펴낸 공상과학소설 *Brave New World*(1932)의 작가로 알려져 있다. 이 작품은 과학과 기계문명의 발전에 대한 맹목적 신뢰가 얼마나 끔찍한 결과를 낳는지를 보여 주는 반유토피아적 주제를 담은 선구적 디스토피아(dystopia) 소설로 평가받는다. 여기 수록한 "Half-Holiday"(1926)는 '말더듬'이라는 신체 결함을 지닌 청년의 좌절된 사랑의 욕구를 그린 단편이다. 언뜻 보면 범상한 이야기지만 말더듬이라는 장애가 암시하듯 소통과 교류가 단절된 현대인들의 소외된 삶과 사랑을 냉소적으로 형상화한 작품이며, 또 그런 점에서 현대사회의 여러 문제에 깊은 관심을 가지고 그 대안을 지속적으로 모색해 온 작가의 평소 문제의식과 일정한 연장선상에 있다고 볼 수 있다.

Half-Holiday

>>~

I

It was Saturday afternoon and fine. In the hazy spring
sunlight London was beautiful, like a city of the imagination.
The lights were golden, the shadows blue and violet.
Incorrigibly hopeful,[1] the sooty trees in the Park[2] were
breaking into leaf;[3] and the new green was unbelievably fresh
and light and aerial,[4] as though the tiny leaves had been cut
out of the central emerald stripe of a rainbow. The miracle, to
all who walked in the Park that afternoon, was manifest. What
had been dead now lived; soot was budding into rainbow
green. Yes, it was manifest. And, moreover, those who

---

1 incorrigibly hopeful: 엄청난 희망을 품고 * incorrigible: 교정할 수 없는,
   제멋대로의, 완강한
2 the Park: 런던 중심부의 대공원 하이드 파크(Hyde Park)를 가리킴.
3 break into leaf: 갑자기 잎을 피우다
4 aerial: 영묘한, 천상의

perceived this thaumaturgical[5] change from death to life were themselves changed. There was something contagious about the vernal[6] miracle. Loving more, the loitering couples under the trees were happier — or much more acutely miserable. Stout men took off their hats and, while the sun kissed their 5 bald heads, made good resolutions — about whisky, about the pretty typist at the office, about early rising. Accosted[7] by spring-intoxicated boys, young girls consented, in the teeth of[8] all their upbringing and their alarm, to go for walks. Middle-aged gentlemen, strolling homeward through the 10 Park, suddenly felt their crusted, business-grimy[9] hearts burgeoning, like these trees, with kindness and generosity. They thought of their wives, thought of them with a sudden gush of affection,[10] in spite of twenty years of marriage. "Must stop on the way back," they said to themselves, "and buy the 15

---

5   thaumaturgical: =miraculous *thaumaturge: 기적을 행하는 사람, 요술쟁이

6   vernal: 봄의

7   accost: 다가가서 말을 걸다

8   in the teeth of: ~에도 굴하지 않고, ~에도 아랑곳없이

9   business-grimy: 일 때가 묻은

10   with a sudden gush of affection: 갑작스럽게 애정이 솟구쳐

missus[11] a little present." What should it be? A box of candied fruits?[12] She liked candied fruits. Or a pot of azaleas? Or... And then they remembered that it was Saturday afternoon. The shops would all be shut. And probably, they thought, sighing, the missus's heart would also be shut; for the missus had not walked under the budding trees. Such is life,[13] they reflected, looking sadly at the boats on the glittering Serpentine,[14] at the playing children, at the lovers sitting, hand in hand, on the green grass. Such is life; when the heart is open, the shops are generally shut. But they resolved nevertheless to try, in future, to control their tempers.[15]

On Peter Brett, as on everyone else who came within their range of influence,[16] this bright spring sunlight and the new-budded trees profoundly worked. They made him feel, all at once, more lonely, more heart-broken than he had ever

---

11 missus : <구어> =missis, wife

12 candied fruits : 설탕 절임 과일

13 Such is life : 인생이란 그런 것이다

14 Serpentine : 하이드 파크 서쪽에 있는 연못으로, 남북 방향으로 길쭉한 'S' 자 모양으로 휘어져 있음. * serpent : 뱀

15 control their temper : 성질을 죽이다, 화를 참다

16 within their range of influence : 그들의 영향권 안에 있는 * 여기서 '그들'은 문장의 주어인 bright spring sunlight and the new-budded trees를 가리킴.

felt before. By contrast with the brightness around him, his soul seemed darker. The trees had broken into leaf; but he remained dead. The lovers walked in couples; he walked alone. In spite of the spring, in spite of the sunshine, in spite of the fact that to-day was Saturday and that to-morrow would be Sunday — or rather because of all these things which should have made him happy and which did make other people happy — he loitered through the miracle of Hyde Park feeling deeply miserable.

As usual, he turned for comfort to his imagination. For example, a lovely young creature would slip on a loose stone[17] just in front of him and twist her ankle. Grown larger than life and handsomer,[18] Peter would rush forward to administer first aid.[19] He would take her in a taxi (for which he had money to pay) to her home — in Grosvenor Square.[20] She turned out to be a peer's daughter. They loved each other....

Or else he rescued a child that had fallen into the Round

---

17 a loose stone : 아무렇게나 놓인 돌
18 Grown larger than life and handsomer : (상상 속에서) 실제보다 키가 더 크고 미남이 되어
19 administer first aid : 응급처치를 하다
20 Grosvenor Square : 런던 서부의 상류 주택지구 * Grosvenor는 [grɔuvnə] 로 읽음.

Pond[21] and so earned the eternal gratitude, and more than the gratitude, of its rich young widowed mother. Yes, widowed; Peter always definitely specified her widowhood. His intentions were strictly honorable. He was still very young and had been well brought up.

Or else there was no preliminary accident. He just saw a young girl sitting on a bench by herself, looking very lonely and sad. Boldly, yet courteously, he approached, he took off his hat, he smiled. "I can see that you're lonely," he said; and he spoke elegantly and with ease, without a trace of his Lancashire accent,[22] without so much as[23] a hint of that dreadful stammer which, in real life, made speech such a torment to him. "I can see that you're lonely. So am I. May I sit down beside you?" She smiled, and he sat down. And then he told her that he was an orphan and that all he had was a married sister who lived in Rochdale. And she said, "I'm an orphan too." And that was a great bond between them. And

---

21   the Round Pond: 하이드 파크의 서쪽 Kensington Garden 중심부에 있는 연못

22   Lancashire accent: Manchester, Liverpool 등이 위치한 잉글랜드 북부지역 특유의 사투리 액센트 ＊아래에 나오는 Rochdale도 잉글랜드 북부지역에 속함.

23   without so much as: ~조차 없이

they told one another how miserable they were. And she began to cry. And then he said, "Don't cry. You've got me." And at that she cheered up a little. And then they went to the pictures together. And finally, he supposed, they got married. But that part of the story was a little dim.

But of course, as a matter of fact, no accidents ever did happen and he never had the courage to tell anyone how lonely he was; and his stammer was something[24] awful; and he was small, he wore spectacles, and nearly always had pimples on his face; and his dark gray suit was growing very shabby and rather short in the sleeves; and his boots, though carefully blacked, looked just as cheap as they really were.

It was the boots which killed his imaginings this afternoon. Walking with downcast eyes, pensively, he was trying to decide what he should say to the peer's lovely young daughter in the taxi on the way to Grosvenor Square, when he suddenly became aware of his alternately striding boots,[25] blackly obtruding[26] themselves through the transparent phantoms

---

24 something : =somewhat
25 alternately striding boots : 번갈아 걸음을 내딛는 양쪽 구두
26 blackly obtruding : 심술궂게 끼어들다 *black : 불길한, 음울한

of his inner life. How ugly they were! And how sadly unlike[27] those elegant and sumptuously shining boots which encase the feet of the rich! They had been ugly enough when they were new; age had rendered them positively repulsive. No boot-trees[28] had corrected the effects of walking, and the uppers,[29] just above the toe-caps,[30] were deeply and hideously wrinkled. Through the polish he could see a network of innumerable little cracks in the parched and shoddy leather.[31] On the outer side of the left boot the toe-cap had come unstitched[32] and had been coarsely sewn up again; the scar was only too visible.[33] Worn by much lacing and unlacing, the eyeholes had lost their black enamel and revealed themselves obtrusively in their brassy nakedness.[34]

　　Oh, they were horrible, his boots; they were disgusting! But

---

27　sadly unlike : 심하게 다른

28　boot-trees : 구둣골

29　uppers : 구두의 갑피(甲皮) ＊보통 복수형으로 사용함.

30　toe-caps : (구두의) 앞닫이 ＊걸을 때 구부러졌다 펴졌다 하는 구두의 앞부분.

31　the parched and shoddy leather : 말라비틀어진 조악한 (구두) 가죽

32　come unstitched : (꿰맨 것이) 풀리다

33　was only too visible : 유감스럽지만 눈에 선명했다

34　in their brassy nakedness : 바탕의 놋쇠가 드러난 상태로

they'd have to last him a long time yet. Peter began to re-make the calculations he had so often and often made before. If he spent three-halfpence less every day on his lunch; if, during the fine weather, he were to walk to the office every morning instead of taking the bus... But however carefully and however 5 often he made his calculations, twenty-seven and sixpence a week always remained twenty-seven and six. Boots were dear; and when he had saved up enough to buy a new pair, there was still the question of his suit. And, to make matters worse, it was spring; the leaves were coming out, the sun shone, and 10 among the amorous couples he walked alone. Reality was too much for him to-day; he could not escape. The boots pursued him whenever he tried to flee, and dragged him back to the contemplation of his misery.

II

The two young women turned out of the crowded walk[35] 15 along the edge of the Serpentine, and struck uphill by a

---

35 walk: 보도, 샛길, 산책로

smaller path in the direction of Watts's statue.[36] Peter followed them. An exquisite perfume lingered in the air behind them. He breathed it greedily and his heart began to beat with unaccustomed violence. They seemed to him marvelous
5 and hardly human beings. They were all that was lovely and unattainable. He had met them walking down there, by the Serpentine, had been overwhelmed by that glimpse of a luxurious and arrogant beauty, had turned immediately and followed them. Why? He hardly knew himself. Merely
10 in order that he might be near them; and perhaps with the fantastic, irrepressible hope that something might happen, some miracle, that should project him into their lives.

Greedily he sniffed their delicate[37] perfume; with a kind of desperation, as though his life depended on it, he looked at
15 them, he studied[38] them. Both were tall. One of them wore a gray cloth coat, trimmed[39] with dark gray fur. The other's coat was all of fur; a dozen or two of ruddily golden foxes[40] had

---

36 Watts's statue : 당대 화가이자 조각가인 George Frederic Watts(1817~
   1904)의 작품 'Physical Energy'로 추정됨.

37 delicate : (빛, 향기, 맛 따위가) 은은한, 부드러운

38 study : 자세히 보다, 유심히 살펴보다

39 trim : 장식하다, 치장하다

40 ruddily golden foxes : 불그레한 황금빛 여우

been killed in order that she might be warm among the chilly shadows of this spring afternoon. One of them wore gray and the other buff-colored[41] stockings. One walked on gray kid,[42] the other on serpent's leather. Their hats were small and close-fitting. A small black French bulldog accompanied them, running now at their heels, now in front of them. The dog's collar was trimmed with brindled[43] wolf's fur that stuck out[44] like a ruff[45] round its black head.

Peter walked so close behind them that, when they were out of the crowd, he could hear snatches[46] of their talk. One had a cooing voice;[47] the other spoke rather huskily. "Such a divine[48] man," the husky voice was saying, "such a really divine man!"

"So Elizabeth told me," said the cooing one.

"Such a perfect party, too," Husky went on. "He kept us

---

41   buff-colored : 담황색의
42   gray kid : 회색 염소 가죽 구두 *kid : 새끼 염소, 새끼 염소 가죽 (구두)
43   brindled : (털이) 얼룩덜룩한
44   stick out : (툭) 튀어나오다, ~을 내밀다
45   ruff : 주름 옷깃
46   snatches : =fragments. 단편, 부서진 조각, 일부분
47   a cooing voice : 달콤한 목소리
48   divine : <구어> 근사한, 훌륭한

laughing the whole evening. Everybody got rather buffy,[49] too. When it was time to go, I said I'd walk and trust to luck[50] to find a taxi on the way. Whereupon he invited me to come and look for a taxi in his heart. He said there were so many there, and all of them disengaged."

They both laughed. The chatter of a party of children who had come up from behind and were passing at this moment prevented Peter from hearing what was said next. Inwardly he cursed the children. Beastly[51] little devils — they were making him lose his revelation. And what a revelation![52] Of how strange, unfamiliar and gaudy[53] a life! Peter's dreams had always been idyllic[54] and pastoral. Even with the peer's daughter he meant to live in the country, quietly and domestically.[55] The world in which there are perfect parties where everybody gets rather buffy and divine men invite young goddesses to look for taxis in their hearts was utterly

---

49 buffy : <속어> =intoxicated. 술 취한

50 trust to luck : 운에 맡기다

51 beastly : 불쾌한, 지겨운

52 What a revelation! : 정말 뜻밖이군! *revelation : 뜻밖의 사실, 놀라운 일

53 gaudy : 번쩍거리는, 화려한

54 idyllic : 목가적인

55 domestically : 가정적으로, 가정에 충실하게

unknown to him. He had had a glimpse of it now; it fascinated him by its exotic and tropical[56] strangeness. His whole ambition was now to enter this gorgeous world, to involve himself, somehow and at all costs,[57] in the lives of these goddesses. Suppose, now, they were both simultaneously to trip over that projecting root and twist their ankles. Suppose... But they both stepped over it in safety. And then, all at once, he saw a hope — in the bulldog.

The dog had left the path to sniff at the base of an elm tree[58] growing a few yards away on the right. It had sniffed, it had growled, it had left a challenging souvenir of its visit[59] and was now indignantly kicking up earth and twigs with its hinder paws[60] against the tree, when a yellow Irish terrier trotted up and began in its turn to sniff, first at the tree, then at the bulldog. The bulldog stopped its scrabbling[61] in the dirt and sniffed at the terrier. Cautiously, the two beasts walked round

---

56 tropical : 열정적인, 격렬한
57 somehow and at all costs : 어떻게 해서든지 무슨 대가를 치르더라도
58 elm tree : 느릅나무
59 left a challenging souvenir of its visit : 개가 오줌을 눈 것을 재미있게 표현한 것임.
60 hinder paws : 뒷발
61 scrabble : (손톱으로) 할퀴다

one another, sniffing and growling as they went. Peter watched them for a moment with a vague and languid[62] curiosity. His mind was elsewhere; he hardly saw the two dogs. Then, in an illuminating flash,[63] it occurred to him that they might begin

to fight. If they fought, he was a made man.[64] He would rush in and separate them, heroically. He might even be bitten. But that didn't matter. Indeed, it would be all the better. A bite would be another claim on the goddesses' gratitude.[65] Ardently, he hoped that the dogs would fight. The awful thing

would be if the goddesses or the owners of the yellow terrier were to notice and interfere before the fight could begin. "Oh God," he fervently prayed, "don't let them call the dogs away from each other now. But let the dogs fight. For Jesus Christ's sake. Amen." Peter had been piously brought up.

The children had passed. The voices of the goddesses once more became audible.

"...Such a fearful bore,"[66] the cooing one was saying. "I can

---

62 languid: 활기 없는, 무감동한

63 in an illuminating flash: 번개처럼, 순식간에

64 a made man: =a successful man

65 claim on the goddesses' gratitude: 여신들의 감사를 요구할 권리

66 a fearful bore: =a fearfully boring man

never move a step without finding him there. And nothing penetrates his hide.[67] I've told him that I hate Jews, that I think he's ugly and stupid and tactless and impertinent and boring. But it doesn't seem to make the slightest difference."

"You should make him useful, at any rate," said Husky.

"Oh, I do," affirmed Coo.

'Well, that's something."[68]

"Something," Coo admitted. "But not much."

There was a pause. "Oh, God," prayed Peter, "don't let them see."

"If only," began Coo meditatively, "if only men would understand that…" A fearful noise of growling and barking violently interrupted her. The two young women turned in the direction from which the sound came.

"Pongo!" they shouted in chorus, anxiously and commandingly. And again, more urgently, "Pongo!"

But their cries were unavailing.[69] Pongo and the yellow terrier were already fighting too furiously to pay any attention.

"Pongo! Pongo!"

---

67 nothing penetrates his hide : 낯가죽이 무척 두꺼운 사람이야
68 that's something : 그만하면 횡재야, 그 정도면 됐어
69 unavailing : 소용없는, 효과 없는

And, "Benny!" the little girl and her stout nurse[70] to whom the yellow terrier belonged as unavailingly shouted. "Benny, come here!"

The moment had come, the passionately anticipated, the richly pregnant moment.[71] Exultantly,[72] Peter threw himself on the dogs. "Get away, you brute,"[73] he shouted, kicking the Irish terrier. For the terrier was the enemy, the French bulldog — *their* French bulldog — the friend whom he had come, like one of the Olympian gods in the *Iliad*,[74] to assist. "Get away!"

In his excitement, he forgot that he had a stammer. The letter G was always a difficult one for him; but he managed on this occasion to shout "Get away" without a trace of hesitation.[75] He grabbed at the dogs by their stumpy tails, by the scruffs[76] of their necks, and tried to drag them apart. From time to

---

70 nurse : 유모, 보모

71 the passionately anticipated, the richly pregnant moment : 애타게 기다려 온 무척 의미심장한 순간 *pregnant : =full of meaning, highly significant

72 exultantly : 크게 기뻐하며

73 brute : <구어> 짐승, 짐승 같은 놈 *cf.* brutal

74 like one of the Olympian gods in the *Iliad* : 앞에 사용한 여신(goddess)의 비유를 이어 감.

75 without a trace of hesitation : 말더듬 흔적이 없이 *hesitation에 '말더듬'이란 의미도 있음.

76 scruff : 목덜미

time he kicked the yellow terrier. But it was the bulldog which bit him. Stupider even than Ajax,[77] the bulldog had failed to understand that the immortal was fighting on his side. But Peter felt no resentment and, in the heat of the moment, hardly any pain. The blood came oozing out of a row of jagged[78] holes in his left hand.

"Ooh!" cried Coo, as though it were her hand that had been bitten.

"Be careful," anxiously admonished Husky. "Be careful."

The sound of their voices nerved[79] him to further efforts. He kicked and he tugged still harder, and at last, for a fraction of a second,[80] he managed to part the angry beasts. For a fraction of a second neither dog had any portion of the other's anatomy[81] in his mouth. Peter seized the opportunity, and catching the French bulldog by the loose skin at the back of his neck, he lifted him, still furiously snapping, growling and

---

77 Ajax: <그리스 신화> 아이아스 ＊트로이 전쟁에 참가한 그리스의 영웅 (Ajax the great)이었으나, 오디세우스와의 불화 끝에 양떼를 군대로 착각하여 베어 죽이고는 제정신이 들어 수치심에 자결한 인물.

78 jagged: 톱니 모양의

79 nerve: 용기를 내게 하다, 힘을 돋우다

80 for a fraction of a second: 아주 잠깐 동안

81 anatomy: =body. 해부학적 조직(구조)

struggling, into the air. The yellow terrier stood in front of him, barking and every now and then leaping up in a frantic effort to snap the dangling black paws of his enemy. But Peter, with the gesture of Perseus[82] raising on high the severed head of the Gorgon,[83] lifted the writhing Pongo out of danger to the highest stretch of his arm. The yellow dog he kept off with his foot; and the nurse and the little girl, who had by this time somewhat recovered their presence of mind,[84] approached the furious animal from behind and succeeded at last in hooking the leash to his collar. His four rigidly planted paws skidding over the grass, the yellow terrier was dragged away by main force,[85] still barking, though feebly — for he was being half strangled by his efforts to escape. Suspended six feet above the ground by the leathery black scruff of his neck, Pongo vainly writhed.[86]

Peter turned and approached the goddesses. Husky had narrow eyes and a sad mouth; it was a thin, tragic-looking

---

82 Perseus: <그리스 신화> 페르세우스
83 Gorgon: <그리스 신화> 세 자매 괴물 *이들 중 막내인 메두사(Medusa)
     가 페르세우스에게 목이 잘려 죽음.
84 presence of mind: 침착, 안정
85 by main force: 강제로
86 writhe: (극심한 고통으로) 온몸을 비틀다, 몸부림치다

face. Coo was rounder,[87] pinker and whiter, bluer-eyed. Peter looked from one to the other and could not decide which was the more beautiful.

He lowered the writhing Pongo. "Here's your dog," was what he wanted to say. But the loveliness of these radiant creatures suddenly brought back all his self-consciousness and with his self-consciousness his stammer. "Here's your..." he began; but could not bring out the dog. D, for Peter, was always a difficult letter.

For all common words beginning with a difficult letter Peter had a number of easier synonyms in readiness. Thus, he always called cats 'pussies,' not out of any affectation of childishness,[88] but because p was more pronounceable than the impossible c. Coal he had to render[89] in the vaguer form of 'fuel.' Dirt,[90] with him, was always 'muck.'[91] In the discovery of synonyms he had become almost as ingenious as those Anglo-Saxon poets who, using alliteration instead

---

87 round : 통통한, 토실토실 살찐
88 out of any affectation of childishness : 어린아이 티를 내어
89 render : 표현하다, 묘사하다
90 dirt : 진흙, 쓰레기, 오물
91 muck : 거름, 퇴비, 오물

of rhyme,[92] were compelled, in their efforts to make (shall we say) the sea begin with the same letter as its waves or its billows, to call it the 'whale-road' or the 'bath of the swans.' But Peter, who could not permit himself the full poetic license[93] of his Saxon ancestors, was reduced sometimes to[94] spelling the most difficult words to which there happened to be no convenient and prosaic[95] equivalent. Thus, he was never quite sure whether he should call a cup a mug or a c, u, p. And since 'ovum'[96] seemed to be the only synonym for egg, he was always reduced to talking of e, g, g' s.

At the present moment, it was the miserable little word 'dog' that was holding him up.[97] Peter had several synonyms for dog. P being a slightly easier letter than d, he could, when not too nervous, say 'pup.' Or if the p's weren't coming easily, he could call the animal, rather facetiously and mock-

---

92 using alliteration instead of rhyme : 각운(脚韻) 대신 두운(頭韻)을 써서
93 poetic license : 시적 허용 ＊시적 효과를 위해 문법에 어긋난 표현이나 어순의 도치, 고어나 신조어 등을 활용하는 파격 용법을 가리킴.
94 was reduced to : 부득이 ~하게 되었다
95 prosaic : 일상적인, 산문적인
96 ovum : 알, 난자
97 hold up : =delay

heroically,[98] a 'hound.'[99] But the presence of the two goddesses was so unnerving that Peter found it as hopelessly impossible to pronounce a p or an h as a d. He hesitated painfully, trying to bring out in turn, first dog, then pup, then hound. His face became very red. He was in an agony.

"Here's your whelp,"[100] he managed to say at last. The word, he was conscious, was a little too Shakespearean for ordinary conversation. But it was the only one which came.

"Thank you most awfully," said Coo.

"You were splendid, really splendid," said Husky. "But I'm afraid you're hurt."

"Oh, it's n-nothing," Peter declared. And twisting his handkerchief round the bitten hand, he thrust it into his pocket.

Coo, meanwhile, had fastened the end of her leash to

---

98 rather facetiously and mock-heroically: 다소 익살맞고 모의영웅시 풍으로 ＊모의영웅시(mock-heroic): 풍자효과를 얻기 위해 사소한 사건이나 주제를 고대 영웅서사시의 문체와 형식을 빌어 과장되게 표현하는 신고전주의 시대의 대표적 풍자문학.

99 hound: <고어, 시어> 개 ＊현대영어에서는 귀족들이 사냥할 때 데리고 다니던 사냥개를 가리킴.

100 whelp: 강아지 ＊일상어로는 잘 쓰지 않으며 경멸조로 '개구쟁이', '불량배'의 뜻이 있음.

Pongo's collar. "You can put him down now," she said.

Peter did as he was told. The little black dog immediately bounded forward in the direction of his reluctantly retreating enemy. He came to the end of his tether with a jerk[101] that brought him up on to his hind legs and kept him, barking, in the position of a rampant lion on a coat of arms.[102]

"But are you sure it's nothing?" Husky insisted. "Let me look at it."

Obediently, Peter pulled off the handkerchief and held out his hand. It seemed to him that all was happening as he had hoped. Then he noticed with horror that the nails were dirty. If only, if only he had thought of washing before he went out! What would they think of him? Blushing, he tried to withdraw his hand. But Husky held it.

"Wait," she said. And then added: "It's a nasty[103] bite."

"Horrid," affirmed Coo, who had also bent over it. "I'm so awfully sorry that my stupid dog should have..."

"You ought to go straight to a chemist,"[104] said Husky,

---

101 with a jerk: 홱, 갑자기
102 a rampant lion on a coat of arms: 문장(紋章)에 그려진 뒷다리로 선 사자
103 nasty: (병 따위가) 심한, 중한
104 chemist: <영국> 약사

interrupting her, "and get him to disinfect it and tie it up."

She lifted her eyes from his hand and looked into his face.

"A chemist," echoed Coo, and also looked up.

Peter looked from one to the other, dazzled equally by the wide-open blue eyes and the narrowed, secret[105] eyes of green. He smiled at them vaguely and vaguely shook his head. Unobtrusively[106] he wrapped up his hand in his handkerchief and thrust it away, out of sight.

"It's n-nothing," he said.

"But you must," insisted Husky.

"You must," cried Coo.

"N-nothing," he repeated. He didn't want to go to a chemist. He wanted to stay with the goddesses.

Coo turned to Husky. "Qu'est-ce qu'on donne à ce petit bonhomme?"[107] she asked, speaking very quickly and in a low voice.

Husky shrugged her shoulders and made a little grimace

---

105 secret: 은밀한, 눈에 잘 보이지 않는
106 unobtrusively: 드러나지 않게, 슬그머니
107 Qu'est-ce qu'on donne à ce petit bonhomme? : =What shall we give this little fellow?

suggestive of uncertainty. "Il serait offensé, peut-être,"[108] she suggested.

"Tu crois?"[109]

Husky stole a rapid glance at[110] the subject of their discussion, taking him in[111] critically from his cheap felt hat to his cheap boots, from his pale, spotty[112] face to his rather dirty hands, from his steel-framed spectacles to his leather watch-guard. Peter saw that she was looking at him and smiled at her with shy, vague rapture. How beautiful she was! He wondered what they had been whispering about together. Perhaps they were debating whether they should ask him to tea. And no sooner had the idea occurred to him than he was sure of it. Miraculously, things were happening just as they happened in his dreams. He wondered if he would have the face to[113] tell them — this first time — that they could look for taxis in his heart.

---

108 Il serait offensé, peut-être : =He will be offended, perhaps

109 Tu crois? : =Do you think so?

110 stole a rapid glance at : ~을 재빠르게 훔쳐보았다

111 taking him in : 그를 유심히 보다 * take in : =notice or see fully

112 spotty : 여드름이 난

113 have the face to : =be bold or rude enough to * face : 태연한 얼굴, 뻔뻔 스러움

Husky turned back to her companion. Once more she shrugged her shoulders. "Vraiment, je ne sais pas,"[114] she whispered.

"Si on lui donnait une livre?"[115] suggested Coo.

Husky nodded. "Comme tu voudras."[116] And while the other turned away to fumble unobtrusively in her purse,[117] she addressed herself to Peter.

"You were awfully brave," she said, smiling.

Peter could only shake his head, blush and lower his eyes from before that steady, self-assured, cool gaze. He longed to look at her; but when it came to the point,[118] he simply could not keep his eyes steadily fixed on those unwavering eyes of hers.

"Perhaps you're used to dogs," she went on. "Have you got one of your own?"

"N-no," Peter managed to say.

"Ah, well, that makes it all the braver,"[119] said Husky.

---

114 Vraiment, je ne sais pas : =In truth, I don't know
115 Si on lui donnait une livre? : =If you gave him a pound?
116 Comme tu voudras : =As you wish
117 fumble unobtrusively in her purse : 은밀하게 자기 지갑을 더듬다
118 when it came to the point : 결정적인 순간에 이르렀을 때
119 that makes it all the braver : 그렇다면 더욱 더 용감하시군요

Then, noticing that Coo had found the money she had been looking for, she took the boy's hand and shook it, heartily. "Well, good-bye," she said, smiling more exquisitely than ever. "We're so awfully grateful to you. Most awfully," she repeated. And as she did so, she wondered why she used that word 'awfully' so often. Ordinarily she hardly ever used it. It had seemed suitable somehow, when she was talking with this creature. She was always very hearty and emphatic and school-boyishly slangy[120] when she was with the lower classes.

"G-g-g..." began Peter. Could they be going, he wondered in an agony, suddenly waking out of his comfortable and rosy dream. Really going, without asking him to tea or giving him their addresses? He wanted to implore them to stop a little longer, to let him see them again. But he knew that he wouldn't be able to utter the necessary words. In the face of Husky's goodbye he felt like a man who sees some fearful catastrophe impending[121] and can do nothing to arrest[122] it. "G-g...," he feebly stuttered. But he found himself shaking hands with the other one before he had got to the end of that

---

120 school-boyishly slangy : 학생같이 속어를 쓰는
121 impending : 임박한
122 arrest : =stop

fatal goodbye.

"You were really splendid," said Coo, as she shook his hand. "Really splendid. And you simply must go to a chemist and have the bite disinfected at once. Goodbye, and thank you very, very much." As she spoke these last words she slipped a neatly folded one-pound note into his palm and with her two hands shut his fingers over it. "Thank you so much," she repeated.

Violently blushing, Peter shook his head. "N-n..." he began, and tried to make her take the note back.

But she only smiled more sweetly. "Yes, yes," she insisted. "Please." And without waiting to hear any more, she turned and ran lightly after Husky, who had walked on, up the path, leading the reluctant Pongo, who still barked and strained heraldically at his leash.[123]

"Well, that's all right," she said, as she came up with[124] her companion.

"He accepted it?" asked Husky.

"Yes, yes," She nodded. Then changing her tone, "Let me

---

123 strained heraldically at his leash : 줄을 잡아당겨 문장에서와 같은 자세를 취했다 *heraldic : 문장(紋章)의, 문장학의

124 came up with : 따라잡았다

see," she went on, "what were we saying when this wretched dog interrupted us?"

"N-no," Peter managed to say at last. But she had already turned and was hurrying away. He took a couple of strides in pursuit;[125] then checked himself. It was no good. It would only lead to further humiliation if he tried to explain. Why, they might even think, while he was standing there, straining to bring out his words,[126] that he had run after them to ask for more. They might slip another pound into his hand and hurry away still faster. He watched them till they were out of sight, over the brow of the hill;[127] then turned back toward the Serpentine.

In his imagination he re-acted the scene, not as it had really happened, but as it ought to have happened. When Coo slipped the note into his hand he smiled and courteously returned it, saying: "I'm afraid you've made a mistake. A quite justifiable mistake, I admit. For I look poor, and indeed I am poor. But I am a gentleman, you know. My father was a doctor in Rochdale. My mother was a doctor's daughter. I

---

125 took a couple of strides in pursuit : 크게 두세 걸음 뒤쫓았다
126 straining to bring out his words : 단어를 찾아내려고 애쓰면서
127 the brow of the hill : 언덕바지, 언덕의 꼭대기

went to a good school till my people[128] died. They died when I was sixteen, within a few months of one another. So I had to go to work before I'd finished my schooling. But you see that I can't take your money." And then, becoming more gallant, personal and confidential,[129] he went on: "I separated those beastly dogs because I wanted to do something for you and your friend. Because I thought you so beautiful and wonderful. So that even if I weren't a gentleman,[130] I wouldn't take your money." Coo was deeply touched by this little speech. She shook him by the hand and told him how sorry she was. And he put her at her ease by assuring her that her mistake had been perfectly comprehensible. And then she asked if he'd care to come along with them and take a cup of tea. And from this point onward Peter's imaginings became vaguer and rosier, till he was dreaming the old familiar dream of the peer's daughter, the grateful widow and the lonely orphan; only there happened to be two goddesses this time,

---

128 my people : 나의 부모

129 becoming more gallant, personal and confidential : 좀 더 의젓하고 친근하고 신뢰할 만한 사이가 되어

130 a gentleman : 여기서는 '계급'으로서 신사를 가리킴.

and their faces, instead of being dim creations of fancy,[131] were real and definite.[132]

But he knew, even in the midst of his dreaming, that things hadn't happened like this. He knew that she had gone before he could say anything; and that even if he had run after them and tried to make his speech of explanation, he could never have done it. For example, he would have had to say that his father was a "medico,"[133] not a doctor (m being an easier letter than d). And when it came to telling them that his people had died, he would have had to say that they had 'perished' — which would sound facetious, as though he were trying to make a joke of it. No, no, the truth must be faced. He had taken the money and they had gone away thinking that he was just some sort of a street loafer,[134] who had risked a bite for the sake of a good tip. They hadn't even dreamed of treating him as an equal.[135] As for asking him to tea and making him their friend...

---

131 dim creations of fancy : 희미한 공상의 산물
132 real and definite : 확실하고 분명한
133 medico : <구어> 의사
134 a street loafer : =a tramp. 부랑자
135 an equal : 대등한 사람

But his fancy was still busy. It struck him that it had been quite unnecessary to make any explanation. He might simply have forced the note back into her hand, without saying a word. Why hadn't he done it? He had to excuse himself for his remissness.[136] She had slipped away too quickly; that was the reason.

Or what if he had walked on ahead of them and ostentatiously[137] given the money to the first street-boy he happened to meet? A good idea, that. Unfortunately it had not occurred to him at the time.

All that afternoon Peter walked and walked, thinking of what had happened, imagining creditable[138] and satisfying alternatives. But all the time he knew that these alternatives were only fanciful. Sometimes the recollection of his humiliation was so vivid that it made him physically wince and shudder.

The light began to fail.[139] In the gray and violet twilight the lovers pressed closer together as they walked, more frankly

---

136 remissness : 실수, 굼뜬 행동
137 ostentatiously : 보란 듯이
138 creditable : 부끄럽지 않은
139 fail : 약해지다, 희미해지다

clasped one another beneath the trees. Strings of yellow lamps blossomed in the increasing darkness. High up in the pale sky overhead, a quarter of the moon made itself visible. He felt unhappier and lonelier than ever.

His bitten hand was by this time extremely painful. He left the Park and walked along Oxford Street till he found a chemist. When his hand had been disinfected and bandaged he went into a tea-shop and ordered a poached e, g, g,[140] a roll, and a mug of mocha, which he had to translate for the benefit of the uncomprehending waitress as a c, u, p of c, o, f, f, e, e.

"You seem to think I'm a loafer or a tout."[141] That's what he ought to have said to her, indignantly and proudly. "You've insulted me. If you were a man, I'd knock you down. Take your dirty money." But then, he reflected, he could hardly have expected them to become his friends, after that. On second thoughts, he decided that indignation would have been no good.

"Hurt your hand?" asked the waitress sympathetically, as she set down his egg and his mug of mocha.

Peter nodded. "B-bitten by a d-d... by a h-h-hound." The

140　a poached e, g, g：=a poached egg. 수란(水卵)
141　tout：유객꾼, 손님잡이

word burst out at last, explosively.

Remembered shame made him blush as he spoke. Yes, they had taken him for a tout; they had treated him as though he didn't really exist, as though he were just an instrument whose services you hired and to which, when the bill had 5 been paid, you gave no further thought. The remembrance of humiliation was so vivid; the realization of it so profound and complete, that it affected not only his mind but his body too. His heart beat with unusual rapidity and violence; he felt sick.[142] It was with the greatest difficulty that he managed to 10 eat his egg and drink his mug of mocha.

Still remembering the painful reality, still feverishly[143] constructing his fanciful alternatives to it,[144] Peter left the tea shop and, though he was very tired, resumed his aimless walking. He walked along Oxford Street as far as the Circus,[145] 15 turned down Regent Street, halted in Piccadilly to look at the

---

142 felt sick : 속이 메스꺼웠다

143 feverishly : 열심히, 적극적으로

144 fanciful alternatives to it : 그것(고통스런 현실)에 대한 기발한 대안들

145 the Circus : =the Oxford Circus ＊이 지점에서 우회전하여 남쪽으로 내려가는 길이 Regent Street이며, 다시 한참 내려가면 Piccadilly Circus가 있음.

epileptically twitching sky signs,[146] walked up Shaftesbury Avenue, and turning southward made his way through by-streets toward the Strand.

In a street near Covent Garden a woman brushed against him.[147] "Cheer up, dearie," she said. "Don't look so glum."[148]

Peter looked at her in astonishment. Was it possible that she should have been speaking to him? A woman — was it possible? He knew, of course, that she was what people called a bad woman.[149] But the fact that she should have spoken to him seemed none the less extraordinary; and he did not connect it, somehow, with her "badness."

"Come along with me," she wheedled.[150]

Peter nodded. He could not believe it was true. She took his arm.

"You got money?" she asked anxiously.

He nodded again.

"You look as though you'd been to a funeral," said the

---

146 the epileptically twitching sky signs : 간질 발작처럼 반짝거리는 옥상 광고
147 brushed against him : 그를 슬쩍 스쳤다
148 glum : 시무룩한, 무뚝뚝한
149 a bad woman : =a streetwalker, a street girl. 매춘부
150 wheedle : 감언으로 꾀다, 속여서 ~시키다

woman.

"I'm l-lonely," he explained. He felt ready to weep. He even longed to weep — to weep and to be comforted. His voice trembled as he spoke.

"Lonely? That's funny. A nice-looking boy like you's got no call[151] to be lonely." She laughed significantly and without mirth.

Her bedroom was dimly and pinkly lighted. A smell of cheap scent and unwashed underlinen haunted the air.

"Wait a tick,"[152] she said, and disappeared through a door into an inner room.

He sat there, waiting. A minute later she returned, wearing a kimono and bedroom slippers. She sat on his knees, threw her arms round his neck and began to kiss him. "Lovey," she said in her cracked voice,[153] "lovey." Her eyes were hard[154] and cold. Her breath smelt of spirits.[155] Seen at close range she was indescribably horrible.

---

151   call : =need

152   Wait a tick : =Wait a moment

153   cracked voice : 쉰 목소리

154   hard : 무표정한

155   spirits : 주정(酒精), 화주(火酒), 독한 술

Peter saw her, it seemed to him, for the first time — saw and completely realized her. He averted his face. Remembering the peer's daughter who had sprained her ankle, the lonely orphan, the widow whose child had tumbled into the Round
5 Pond; remembering Coo and Husky, he untwined her arms, he pushed her away from him, he sprang to his feet.

"S-sorry," he said. "I must g-g... I'd forgotten something. I...." He picked up his hat and moved toward the door.

The woman ran after him and caught him by the arm. "You
10 young devil, you," she screamed. Her abuse was horrible and filthy. "Asking a girl and then trying to sneak away[156] without paying. Oh, no you don't, no you don't. You...."

And the abuse began again.

Peter dipped his hand into his pocket, and pulled out Coo's
15 neatly folded note. "L-let me g-go," he said as he gave it her.

While she was suspiciously unfolding it, he hurried away, slamming the door behind him, and ran down the dark stairs, into the street.

---

156 sneak away : 도망가다, 달아나다

작품 해설

1. Peter의 좌절된 로맨스

Peter Brett의 좌절된 로맨스는 그 자체로 충분한 보편성을 지닌다. 찬란한 봄날 Hyde Park를 거니는 행복한 연인들의 평화로운 정경에도 불구하고, 그 속에는 소외된 인간들 역시 존재하게 마련이다. 갑작스런 봄의 충동에 문득 아내에 대한 애정이 되살아난 중년의 사나이도 다시 까닭 모를 좌절감에 사로잡히듯이, 겉보기에는 멀쩡하지만 그들은 모두 외로운 사람이다. Peter도 그 외로운 군상 중의 하나일 뿐, 그들의 외로움은 주변의 사람과 풍경이 찬란할수록 더욱 초라해진다.

그런 점에서 Peter의 습관적 공상은 생생한 현실감을 지닌다. 기적과도 같은 로맨스를 갈구하는 Peter의 공상이 얼마나 간절한지 충분히 납득할 수 있기 때문이다. 공상의 세계야말로 외로운 청년 Peter에게 유일한 탈출구였던 것이다. 하지만 안타깝게도 Peter의 공상이 현실성을 지니는 것만큼 그 꿈의 좌절 역시 충분한 개연성을 지닌다. 사랑과 꿈의 성취는 누구나 쉽게 누릴 수 있는 일상이 아니기 때문이다. Hyde Park의 화사한 햇살 속에 시작한 드라마는 거리의 여인이 서성이는 어두운 뒷골목에서 막을 내림으로써 Peter의 좌절을 더욱 드라마틱하게 보여 준다.

Peter의 외로움이 더욱 초라한 것은 그 같은 쓰라린 실패에도 불구하고 그에게는 거리의 여인에게 돈을 주고 하룻밤을 보낼 만한 용기(?)마저 없다는 사실이다. 마지막 순간에 떠올린 상상 속의 여인들 덕분에 그는 거리의 여인을 뿌리치고 그녀의 방을 뛰쳐나온다. 도회의 어두운 뒷골목에서 자신을 소진시키기에 그는 아직 너무나 정결하며, 또 견고한 내면을 가진 사람이다.

2. Peter의 말더듬

Peter의 지독한 외로움이 독자들의 공감을 이끌어 내는 보편적 상황이라면, 말더듬은 그를 구체적 개인으로 만드는 개성적 정황에 해당한다. 외로움은 무엇보다도 소통과 교류의 결핍을 의미하며, 말더듬은 이 결핍을 가장 강렬하고 압축적으로 나타내는 징후이기 때문이다. 다소 우스꽝스럽게 그려지기는 했지만 발음이 편한 동의어를 찾아 헤매는 Peter의 절박함은 소통을 향한 그의 욕구가 얼마나 간절한지를 생생하게 보여 준다. 여신과도 같은 여인 Coo가 쥐어 주는 1파운드 지폐를 억지로 받아들지만, Peter는 그 순간의 치욕을 표현하지 못하고 고통스럽게 말을 더듬을 뿐이다. 말더듬은 Peter의 고독과 소외를 필연으로 만드는 동인(動因)이며, 그는 이 상황을 다시 공상 속에서 복기하며 분노하고 또 좌절할 수밖에 없다.

3. 반공일과 Peter의 해진 구두

기록에 의하면 영국의 숙련노동자는 대략 1870년경부터 토요일을 '반공일'(half-holiday)로 쉴 수 있었고, 대부분의 노동자들이 토요일을 반공일로 쉬게 된 것은 1890년경이라고 한다. 이때부터 주말(weekend)이라는 개념이 생겨났다고 하는데, 이와 같은 휴일 제도의 변화는 고스란히 영국 노동운동이 이룩한 중요한 성과의 한 장이다. 따라서 넓게 보아 이 소설 도입부에 그려진 바, Hyde Park의 평화로운 정경 속에서 반공일 오후의 여유를 향유하는 시민들의 풍경은 산업혁명 이후 영국 경제의 발전과 이에 바탕을 둔 사회적·문화적 풍요를 과시하는 상징적 한 장면으로 손색이 없다.

그런 점에서 작품 제목의 '반공일'은 새삼스러운 주목을 요한다. 해진 구두로 상징되는 Peter의 가난은 바로 이 지점에서 개인의 문제가 아니라 당대적 함의로 이어지기 때문이다. 반공일 오후 Hyde Park를 방황하는 가난한 청년의 외로움은 발전과 번영의 주변부에서 소외되고 고립된 개인의 초상으로 읽기에 부족함이 없다. 그에게 결정적 좌절을 가져온 두 귀부인과의 조우, 그리고 그들의 두 마리 강아지를 둘러싼 처절한(?) 에피소드는 Peter와 그들을 갈라놓은 계급적 장벽이 얼마나 높은지 생생하게 보여 준다. 나아가 여인들의 불어 사용은 말더듬 정도가 아니라 그들과 Peter의 소통이 원천적으로 불가능했음을 새삼 확인시켜 준다. 요컨대 그 사건은 Peter에게는 비극이었지만 그들에게는 희극이었을 뿐이다.

4. Peter의 자기풍자

두 마리 강아지를 둘러싼 에피소드가 다소 우스꽝스럽게 그려지면서 Peter의 드라마는 계급적인 시각을 넘어서 또 다른 맥락을 떠올린다. 장황하게 묘사된 강아지 에피소드에 슬그머니 풍자의 어조가 실려 있기 때문이다. 스토리가 전개되면서 Peter는 이제 동정의 대상에서 조금씩 풍자의 대상으로 변모하고 있는 것이다. 그런 점에서 Peter의 드라마는 가난한 말더듬이 청년의 좌절된 로맨스인 동시에 현대사회의 고립되고 소외된 개인의 자기풍자적 기행(奇行)이라는 이중적 의미를 띠게 된다. 물론 기적과도 같은 로맨스를 향한 Peter의 간절한 욕망은 고립과 소외를 넘어 진정한 인간적 교류를 갈구하는 염원으로 이해해야 한다. 다만 거기에 덧붙여 그의 말더듬과 습관적 공상, 무력감, 끝없는 내면으로의 도피는 대화와 소통이 불가능해진 시대, 곧 현대적 풍경에 대한 은유(metaphor)로 폭넓게 읽어 내는 것이 이 작품에 대한 온당한 평가일 것이다.

5. 최재서의 번역 "반공일"

이 단편이 작품집 *Two or Three Graces*에 발표된 것이 1926년이었는데, 한국의 초기 영문학자 최재서는 1934년 2월 이를 "반공일"이라는 제목으로 <조선일보> 연재를 통해 번역해 낸다. 영국에서 출판된 작품이 10년도 되지 않아 식민지 조선의 일간신문에 발표된다는 점에서 다소 놀라운 일인데, 최재서의 모더니스틱한 취향이 이 작품의 번역에 작용한 것으로 보인다. 아래에 인용된 최재서 번역본의 첫 단락에서 국한문 혼용에 가까운 당대의 문체를 읽는 신기함과 재미를 맛볼 수 있다.

"봄날이 화창한 반공일 오후이엇다. 안개가 자욱한 봄 해볏 아레 런돈(倫敦)은 꿈나라의 장안가티 아름다웟다. 해가 쪼히는 곳은 황금빗이요 그 늘진 곳은 담자색(淡紫色)이엇다. 것잡을 수 업는 희망에 넘치여 공원(하

이드파아크)의 그름탄 나무들은 새눈을 뽑고 잇섯다. 그리고 새로운 잔디
밧은 마침 그 풀닙들을 무지개의 맨가운데의 에메랄드 대(帶)에서나 따 온
듯이 청신(淸新)하고 경(輕)쾌하엿다."

영미 명작 단편선_6

The Ant and the Grasshopper

William Somerset Maugham

"The Ant and the Grasshopper"(1924)는 William Somerset Maugham(1874~1965)의 또 다른 대표작으로, 이솝 우화 "개미와 베짱이"의 제목과 구조를 그대로 빌려오되 성실과 근면의 중요성을 강조하는 원작의 교훈을 거꾸로 뒤집어 풍자하고 비판하는 패러디 작품이다. 단편소설보다 더 짧은 작품을 가리키는 '한뼘소설'(掌篇, short-short story)로 불러야 할 만큼 길이가 짧지만, 삶의 본질에 관한 꽤나 무거운 주제를 다루고 있다는 점에서 깊은 사색을 요구하는 작품이다. 앞의 "The Luncheon"에서 확인한 바 있는 Maugham 특유의 유머와 위트는 이 작품에서도 여전히 빛을 잃지 않고 있다.

The Ant and the Grasshopper

When I was a very small boy I was made to learn by heart[1] certain of the fables of La Fontaine,[2] and the moral of each was carefully explained to me. Among those I learnt was 'The Ant and the Grasshopper', which is devised to bring home to[3] the young the useful lesson that in an imperfect world industry is rewarded and giddiness[4] punished. In this admirable fable (I apologise for telling something which everyone is politely, but inexactly, supposed to know) the ant spends a laborious summer gathering its winter store; while the grasshopper sits on a blade of grass singing to the sun. Winter comes and

---

1 learn by heart : 암기하다
2 the fables of La Fontaine : 프랑스 작가 라퐁텐(1621~1695)은 이솝우화 (*Aesop's Fables*)를 기초로 하여 많은 우화를 펴냈는데, "개미와 베짱이"도 그중의 한 편이다. 특히 우화를 훌륭한 운문으로 펴냈다는 점에서 높은 문학사적 평가를 받는다.
3 bring home to : ~에게 절실히 느끼게 하다
4 giddiness : 경솔함, 경박함, 어지러움

the ant is comfortably provided for, but the grasshopper has
an empty larder:[5] he goes to the ant and begs for a little food.
Then the ant gives him her classic answer:

"What were you doing in the summer time?"

"Saving your presence,[6] I sang, I sang all day, all night."

"You sang. Why, then go and dance."

I do not ascribe it to perversity[7] on my part, but rather to
the inconsequence[8] of childhood, which is deficient in moral
sense, that I could never quite reconcile myself to[9] the lesson.
My sympathies were with the grasshopper and for some
time I never saw an ant without putting my foot on it. In this
summary[10] (and, as I have discovered since, entirely human)
fashion I sought to express my disapproval of prudence and
commonsense.

I could not help thinking[11] of this fable when the other day
I saw George Ramsay lunching by himself in a restaurant.

---

5 larder: 고기 저장소, 식료품실

6 Saving your presence: 이런 말씀 드려 죄송합니다만

7 perversity: 심술궂은 마음, 외고집

8 inconsequence: 모순, 비논리성

9 reconcile myself to: ~을 (체념하고) 받아들이다

10 summary: 간결한, 요약한

11 could not help thinking: ~라고 생각하지 않을 수 없었다

I never saw anyone wear an expression of such deep gloom. He was staring into space. He looked as though the burden of the whole world sat on his shoulders. I was sorry for him: I suspected at once that his unfortunate[12] brother had been causing trouble again. I went up to him and held out my hand.

"How are you?" I asked.

"I'm not in hilarious spirits," he answered.

"Is it Tom again?"

He sighed.

"Yes, it's Tom again."

"Why don't you chuck[13] him? You've done everything in the world for him. You must know by now that he's quite hopeless."

I suppose every family has a black sheep.[14] Tom had been a sore trial[15] to his for twenty years. He had begun life decently enough: he went into business, married and had two children. The Ramsays were perfectly respectable people and there was every reason to suppose that Tom Ramsay would have a

---

12 unfortunate: 유감스러운, 한심한
13 chuck: 버리다, 팽개치다, 포기하다
14 black sheep: 골칫덩어리, 말썽꾼
15 a sore trial: 혹독한 시련

useful and honourable career. But one day, without warning, he announced that he didn't like work and that he wasn't suited for marriage. He wanted to enjoy himself. He would listen to no expostulations.[16] He left his wife and his office. He had a little money and he spent two happy years in the various capitals of Europe. Rumours of his doings reached his relations from time to time and they were profoundly shocked. He certainly had a very good time. They shook their heads and asked what would happen when his money was spent. They soon found out: he borrowed. He was charming and unscrupulous.[17] I have never met anyone to whom it was more difficult to refuse a loan. He made a steady income from his friends and he made friends easily. But he always said that the money you spent on necessities was boring; the money that was amusing to spend was the money you spent on luxuries. For this he depended on his brother George. He did not waste his charm on him. George was a serious man and insensible to such enticements.[18] George was respectable.

---

16 expostulations : 훈계, 충고
17 unscrupulous : 부도덕한, 뻔뻔스런, 무원칙한
18 enticements : 유혹, 꾐, 미끼

Once or twice he fell to[19] Tom's promises of amendment[20] and gave him considerable sums in order that he might make a fresh start. On these Tom bought a motorcar and some very nice jewellery. But when circumstances forced George to realise that his brother would never settle down and he washed his hands of[21] him, Tom, without a qualm,[22] began to blackmail him. It was not very nice for a respectable lawyer to find his brother shaking cocktails behind the bar of his favourite restaurant or to see him waiting on the box-seat[23] of a taxi outside his club. Tom said that to serve in a bar or to drive a taxi was a perfectly decent occupation, but if George could oblige him with[24] a couple of hundred pounds he didn't mind for the honour of the family giving it up. George paid.

Once Tom nearly went to prison. George was terribly upset. He went into the whole discreditable affair.[25] Really Tom had

---

19 fall to : ~에게 무너지다

20 amendment : 교정, 개심

21 wash one's hands of : =abandon. ~와의 관계를 끊다

22 without a qualm : =without a blink or qualm. 태연히, 일말의 망설임도 없이 *qualm : 양심의 가책, 불안감, 거리낌

23 box-seat : (마차의) 마부석 *여기서는 '운전석'의 의미.

24 oblige him with : 그에게 은혜를 베풀다, 친절하게 대하다

25 He went into the whole discreditable affair : 그는 이 수치스런 사건 전말을

gone too far. He had been wild, thoughtless and selfish, but he had never before done anything dishonest, by which George meant illegal; and if he were prosecuted he would assuredly be convicted. But you cannot allow your only brother to go to gaol. The man Tom had cheated, a man called Cronshaw, was vindictive. He was determined to take the matter into court; he said Tom was a scoundrel and should be punished. It cost George an infinite deal of trouble and five hundred pounds to settle the affair. I have never seen him in such a rage as when he heard that Tom and Cronshaw had gone off together to Monte Carlo[26] the moment they cashed the cheque. They spent a happy month there.

For twenty years Tom raced[27] and gambled, philandered[28] with the prettiest girls, danced, ate in the most expensive restaurants, and dressed beautifully. He always looked as if he had just stepped out of a bandbox.[29] Though he was forty-six you would never have taken him for more than thirty-five.

조사해 보았다

26 Monte Carlo : 모나코 동북부의 휴양지
27 race : 경마에 몰두하다
28 philander : 여자를 쫓아다니다, 엽색하다
29 looked as if he had just stepped out of a bandbox : 멋지게 차려입고 있었
    다 *a bandbox : (모자 따위를 넣는) 판지 상자

He was a most amusing companion and though you knew he was perfectly worthless you could not but enjoy his society. He had high spirits, an unfailing gaiety and incredible charm. I never grudged the contributions[30] he regularly levied on me for the necessities of his existence. I never lent him fifty pounds without feeling that I was in his debt.[31] Tom Ramsay knew everyone and everyone knew Tom Ramsay. You could not approve of[32] him, but you could not help liking him.

Poor George, only a year older than his scapegrace[33] brother, looked sixty. He had never taken more than a fortnight's holiday in the year for a quarter of a century. He was in his office every morning at nine-thirty and never left it till six. He was honest, industrious and worthy. He had a good wife, to whom he had never been unfaithful even in thought, and four daughters to whom he was the best of fathers. He made a point of[34] saving a third of his income and his plan

---

30 contributions: 보험료, 세금, 분담금
31 I never lent him fifty pounds without feeling that I was in his debt: 나는 그에게 50파운드를 빌려줄 때마다 내가 그에게 빚지고 있다는 생각이 들었다
32 approve of: =agree with or support someone or something
33 scapegrace: 망나니, 건달, 개구쟁이
34 make a point of: ~을 규칙으로 하다, 반드시 ~하다

was to retire at fifty-five to a little house in the country where he proposed to cultivate his garden and play golf. His life was blameless. He was glad that he was growing old because Tom was growing old too. He rubbed his hands and said:

"It was all very well when Tom was young and good-looking, but he's only a year younger than I am. In four years he'll be fifty. He won't find life so easy then. I shall have thirty thousand pounds by the time I'm fifty. For twenty-five years I've said that Tom would end in the gutter.[35] And we shall see how he likes that. We shall see if it really pays best to work or be idle."

Poor George! I sympathized with him. I wondered now as I sat down beside him what infamous thing Tom had done. George was evidently very much upset.

"Do you know what's happened now?" he asked me.

I was prepared for the worst. I wondered if Tom had got into the hands of the police at last. George could hardly bring himself to speak.

"You're not going to deny that all my life I've been hardworking, decent, respectable and straightforward. After

---

35 gutter: 하수도, 시궁창, 빈민굴

a life of industry and thrift I can look forward to retiring on a small income in gilt-edged securities.[36] I've always done my duty in that state of life in which it has pleased Providence to place me."[37]

"True."

"And you can't deny that Tom has been an idle, worthless, dissolute[38] and dishonourable rogue. If there were any justice he'd be in the workhouse."[39]

"True."

George grew red in the face.

"A few weeks ago he became engaged to a woman old enough to be his mother. And now she's died and left him everything she had. Half a million pounds, a yacht, a house in London and a house in the country."

George Ramsay beat his clenched fist on the table.

"It's not fair, I tell you; it's not fair. Damn it, it's not fair."

---

36 gilt-edged securities : 영국 중앙은행(Bank of England)에서 발행하는 낮은 이율의 안정적인 채권 ＊가장자리의 금박으로 인해 이런 이름이 붙음.

37 in that state of life in which it has pleased Providence to place me : 신께서 즐거이 내게 정해 주신 자리에서

38 dissolute : 방탕한

39 workhouse : 구빈원

I could not help it.[40] I burst into a shout of laughter as I looked at George's wrathful face, I rolled in my chair; I very nearly fell on the floor. George never forgave me. But Tom often asked me to excellent dinners in his charming house in Mayfair,[41] and if he occasionally borrows a trifle from me, 5 that is merely from force of habit. It is never more than a sovereign.[42]

40　I could not help it : 나는 어쩔 수 없었다

41　Mayfair : 런던 Hyde Park 동쪽의 고급 주택지구

42　sovereign : (옛 영국의) 1파운드 금화

작품 해설

1. Carpe Diem

이솝우화 "개미와 베짱이"는 성실과 근면이 얼마나 중요한지 일깨우는 익숙한 교훈담이다. 하지만 단편소설 "개미와 베짱이"의 서술자는 원전 우화가 제시하는 고전적 메시지를 대놓고 비웃는다. 무려 20년을 베짱이처럼 무책임하게 놀아난 동생 Tom에게 어느 날 엄청난 행운이 찾아오고, 서술자는 그 행운에 분개하는 형 George의 탄식을 조롱하며 동생의 편을 들어준다. 흥진비래(興盡悲來), 고진감래(苦盡甘來)의 상식과 교훈이 유머러스하게 뒤집어지면서, 독자들은 새삼 삶의 본질에 내재한 아이러니와 만나게 된다. 평생을 개미처럼 일하며 안락하고 평화로운 노년을 꿈꾸어 온 모범생 형은 이제 나이보다 열 살이나 넘게 늙어 보이는 초라한 모습으로 전락해 있을 뿐이다. 삶은 교과서처럼 전개되는 것이 아니다. Somerset Maugham의 주인공들은 종종 상식과 합리의 세계를 넘어 전개되는 삶의 신비로움, 아이러니에 주목하도록 하는데, 이 작품도 그중의 하나이다.

이른바 '카르페 디엠 철학'(the philosophy of Carpe Diem)으로 불리는 베짱이의 논리는 사실 서양 문화와 전통에서는 낯설지 않다. 영어로는 Seize the day!(좀 더 구체적으로는 Enjoy the moment!)라는 말로 번역

되는 이 경구는 요컨대 불확실한 미래에 기대지 말고 지금, 현재의 시간을 즐기고 향유하라는 것이다. 어느 날 갑자기 가족과 직장을 팽개치고 오로지 자기 자신만을 위해 살기로 작정한 Tom은 이 경구의 확실한 실천자인 셈이다. 이 말의 기원은 로마 시인 호라티우스(Horace, 65~8 B.C.)까지 거슬러 올라가는데, 엄밀히 말해서 이 어구의 원래 의미가 향락주의나 쾌락주의적 입장과는 거리가 멀다는 점도 기억할 필요가 있다. 호라티우스의 원전에 따르면 '카르페 디엠'은 '인생의 유한성(mortality)을 기억하고 현재에 더욱 충실하라'는 뜻에 가깝기 때문이다. 즉, 삶의 유한성을 강조하는 데 초점이 있는 것이다. 심지어 그 말 속에 그래야 더 나은 내일을 기대할 수 있다는 의미까지 함축하고 있어서 이 어구의 통상적 용례는 오독에서 비롯되었다고 주장하는 이들도 있다.

2. George의 도덕적 오만

엄격히 말해 한 편의 단편소설로서 이 작품의 핵심구조는 '카르페 디엠 철학'의 논증이 아니라 베짱이 Tom의 행운에 분개하는 개미 George의 내면심리에 초점이 맞춰져 있다. 서술자의 언급대로 "그의 삶은 한 점 흠이 없었고"(His life was blameless.), 그는 성실과 근면 그 자체였다. 그는 동생에게 찾아온 엄청난 행운을 간명하게 요약하고 비난한다. "분명히 말하는데, 그건 공정하지 않아. 공정하지 않다고. 제기랄, 그건 공정하지 않아."(It's not fair, I tell you; it's not fair. Damn it, it's not fair.) 그는 정의(justice)를 요구하고 있다.

문제는 일견 합당해 보이는 형의 불만에 서술자가 동의하지 않는다는 것이다. 어떤 맥락에서 그가 동생 편을 드는지는 분명치 않다. 일차적으로는 교과서적인 삶을 살아온 형의 논리, 곧 그의 철저한 인생설계, 빈틈없는 계산, 질식할 것 같은 삶의 규율에 질려 버린 것으로 추정된다. 변호사 George는 평생을 그렇게 살아온 사람이기 때문이다. 그런데 보다 더 큰 문제는 동생의 일탈과 방종을 지켜보는 그의 태도에 슬그머니 도덕적 오만이 개입해 있다는 사실이다. 사실 동생에게 찾아온 행운 때문에 형이 피해를 본 것은 없고, 오히려 이제 동생이 그에게 손을 벌리지 않을 것이기 때문에 다행이라고 할 수도 있다. 그런데도 형의 협소한 정의감은 동생이 구빈원에서 비참한 말년을 보내야 마땅하다고 규정한다. 인과응보의 벌을 받아 결국 시궁창에서 인생을 마무리지어야 한다는 것이다. 이와 같이 옹졸한 판단의 배경에는 자신의 도덕적 우위에 대한 George의 과도한 오만이 있다. 서술자는 그 오만을 지적하고 싶은 것이다. 요컨대 시뻘게진 얼굴로 탁자를 내리치는 George의 분노 앞에서 폭소를 터뜨리며 의자 위를 구르는 서술자의 태도는 그의 도덕적 오만에 대한 조롱이며 풍자이다.

3. 탕자의 비유(the prodigal son)

기독교인이 아니라도 이쯤 되면 어렵지 않게 『신약성서』 누가복음(15: 11~32)에 나오는 '탕자의 비유'를 떠올리게 된다. Tom에게 찾아온 행운을 아버지의 용서와 잔치로 바꾸어 놓으면 두 이야기는 거의 동일한 구조를 보이기 때문이다. 흥미로운 것은 두 이야기 모두 종결부에서 동생의 행운과 사면에 분개하는 형의 심리와 논리에 주목한다는 점이다. 차이가 있다면 '탕자의 비유'에서는 형의 분노를 잃어버린 아들에 대한 아버지(곧 하느님)의 한없는 용서와 사랑으로 해결하는 반면에,

"The Ant and the Grasshopper"에서는 형의 도덕적 오만에 대한 조롱과 풍자로 마무리를 짓는다. 후자 역시 넓은 의미의 섭리 혹은 질서에 대한 암시라고 할 수도 있을 터인데, 두 이야기 모두 좁은 의미의 정의가 지니는 한계에 대한 문제 제기라는 점은 명백하다.

영미 명작 단편선_7

The Boarding House

James Joyce

20세기 최고의 영국소설가로 꼽히는 James Joyce(1882~ 1941)는 이른바 '의식의 흐름'(the stream of consciousness) 기법 을 대표하는 모더니스트로 알려져 있지만, 단편소설 모음집인 초기작 *Dubliners*(1914)는 자연주의적인 성향을 띤다. "The Boarding House"는 *Dubliners*에 실린 15편의 작품 중 한 편 으로, 덫에 걸린 듯 꼼짝없이 원하지 않는 여자와 결혼할 수밖 에 없는 청년의 우울한 이야기를 사실적으로 그려 내고 있다. *Dubliners*의 수록작품들은 당대 아일랜드 사회의 갑갑하고 암 울한 분위기를 성공적으로 재현하고 있는데, 이 작품을 비롯한 15편의 단편은 개별적으로도 훌륭한 작품이지만 전체적으로 완결된 한 편의 장편소설로 읽어도 좋을 만큼 정교한 짜임새를 보여 준다.

The Boarding House

Mrs. Mooney was a butcher's daughter. She was a woman who was quite able to keep things to herself:[1] a determined woman. She had married her father's foreman and opened a butcher's shop near Spring Gardens. But as soon as his father-in-law was dead Mr. Mooney began to go to the devil.[2] He drank, plundered[3] the till,[4] ran headlong into debt. It was no use making him take the pledge:[5] he was sure to break out again a few days after. By fighting his wife in the presence of customers and by buying bad meat he ruined his business.

---

1 keep things to herself: 일을 혼자서 처리하다
2 go to the devil: =fall into ruin. 몰락하다, 타락하다
3 plunder: 노략질하다, 훔치다
4 till: (상점 계산대의) 돈 서랍
5 take the pledge: 금주(禁酒) 맹세를 하다 *pledge: '맹세, 보증, 서약'이라는 일반적인 뜻이 있지만 여기서는 '금주 맹세'를 뜻함.

One night he went for[6] his wife with the cleaver[7] and she had to sleep in a neighbour's house.

After that they lived apart. She went to the priest and got a separation from him with care of the children.[8] She would give him neither money nor food nor house-room; and so he was obliged to enlist himself as a sheriff's man.[9] He was a shabby stooped little drunkard with a white face and a white moustache and white eyebrows, pencilled[10] above his little eyes, which were pink-veined and raw;[11] and all day long he sat in the bailiff's[12] room, waiting to be put on a job.[13] Mrs. Mooney, who had taken what remained of her money out of the butcher business and set up a boarding

---

6 go for : =attack. 맹렬히 공격하다
7 cleaver : 푸줏간에서 쓰는 큰 칼
8 with care of the children : 아이들을 맡는 조건으로
9 enlist himself as a sheriff's man : 시행정관의 일꾼으로 일하다 *enlist :
   모병하다, 입대시키다
10 pencilled : 연필로 그린 듯한 *앞의 eyebrows를 수식하는 말로, pencil에
   '눈썹을 그리다'라는 뜻이 있음.
11 pink-veined and raw : 핏발이 서고 상스러운
12 bailiff : 집행관 *sheriff 아래의 사법관으로 영장 송달, 압류 집행 등을 맡
   은 관리
13 to be put on a job : 일거리가 생겨 출동하다 *put : (어떤 방향으로) 움직
   이다, 출동시키다

house in Hardwicke Street, was a big imposing[14] woman. Her house had a floating population made up of tourists[15] from Liverpool and the Isle of Man and, occasionally, *artistes*[16] from the music halls. Its resident population[17] was made up of

5 clerks[18] from the city. She governed the house cunningly and firmly, knew when to give credit,[19] when to be stern and when to let things pass. All the resident young men spoke of her as *The Madam.*[20]

Mrs. Mooney's young men paid fifteen shillings a week

10 for board and lodgings[21] (beer or stout at dinner excluded). They shared in common tastes and occupations and for this reason they were very chummy[22] with one another. They discussed with one another the chances of favourites and

---

14 imposing: 당당한, 위압적인

15 a floating population made up of tourists: 여행객들로 이루어진 유동인구

16 *artiste*: (특히 영국영어로) 예능인, 연예인(가수, 무용가, 배우 등)

17 resident population: (앞의 floating population과 구별되는) 장기 투숙객

18 clerk: 일반적인 '서기, 사무원'이라기보다는 '점원'을 가리킴.

19 give credit: 외상을 주다

20 *The Madam*: 부인을 가리키는 정중한 호칭이므로 투숙객들이 그녀를 함부로 대하지 못하였다는 뜻 * 이 말에는 '(사창가의) 포주'란 뜻도 있으므로 작품 이해와 관련하여 기억해 두어야 함.

21 board and lodging: 식사 및 숙박

22 chummy: =friendly * chum: 친구, 동료, 동무

outsiders.[23] Jack Mooney, the Madam's son, who was clerk to a commission agent[24] in Fleet Street, had the reputation of being a hard case.[25] He was fond of using soldiers' obscenities: usually he came home in the small hours.[26] When he met his friends he had always a good one[27] to tell them and he was always sure to be on to[28] a good thing — that is to say, a likely[29] horse or a likely artiste. He was also handy with the mits[30] and sang comic songs. On Sunday nights there would often be a reunion[31] in Mrs. Mooney's front drawing-room. The music-hall artistes would oblige;[32] and Sheridan played waltzes and polkas and vamped[33] accompaniments. Polly Mooney, the Madam's daughter, would also sing. She sang:

---

23 favorites and outsiders : (경마에서) 인기 있는 말과 승산이 없는 말

24 a commission agent : 거간꾼, 중매인

25 a hard case : 불량배, 개전의 정이 없는 죄인

26 the small hours : (자정이 막 지난) 심야, 한밤중

27 a good one : =a good thing, person, or story

28 be on to : (사실 등을) 잘 알고 있다

29 likely : =promising. 가망 있는, 유망한

30 handy with the mits : 주먹 솜씨가 있는 *mits : <속어> =mitts, hands. 주먹, 손

31 reunion : 친목회, 동창회, 모임, 회식

32 oblige : 호의를 보이다, 은혜를 베풀다

33 vamp : =improvise. (노래, 춤 등에) 즉석 반주를 붙이다

I'm a ... naughty girl.

You needn't sham:

You know I am.

⁵ Polly was a slim girl of nineteen; she had light soft hair and a small full mouth.³⁴ Her eyes, which were grey with a shade of green through them, had a habit of glancing upwards when she spoke with anyone, which made her look like a little perverse madonna. Mrs. Mooney had first sent her daughter ¹⁰ to be a typist in a corn-factor's³⁵ office but, as a disreputable sheriff's man used to come every other day to the office, asking to be allowed to say a word to his daughter, she had taken her daughter home again and set her to do housework. As Polly was very lively the intention was to give her the run of ¹⁵ the young men.³⁶ Besides young men like to feel that there is a young woman not very far away. Polly, of course, flirted with the young men but Mrs. Mooney, who was a shrewd judge,³⁷

---

34 full mouth : 통통한 입

35 a corn-factor : 곡물 중개인

36 give her the run of the young men : 그녀로 하여금 청년들과 놀게 하다
   *run은 '출입, 사용의 자유'를 의미함 *cf.* He had the *run* of Mary's house.
   (그는 메리의 집에 자유로이 출입하였다.)

37 a shrewd judge : 예리한 감식가

knew that the young men were only passing the time away:[38] none of them meant business.[39] Things went on so for a long time and Mrs. Mooney began to think of sending Polly back to typewriting when she noticed that something was going on between Polly and one of the young men. She watched the 5 pair and kept her own counsel.[40]

Polly knew that she was being watched, but still[41] her mother's persistent silence could not be misunderstood. There had been no open complicity[42] between mother and daughter, no open understanding[43] but, though people in the 10 house began to talk of the affair,[44] still Mrs. Mooney did not intervene. Polly began to grow a little strange in her manner and the young man was evidently perturbed. At last, when she judged it to be the right moment, Mrs. Mooney intervened.

---

38 pass away : (시간을) 보내다

39 mean business : <구어> =be serious. 진심이다, 진정이다

40 kept her own counsel : 자신의 생각을 남에게 털어놓지 않았다, 혼자 궁리 하였다

41 still : 그럼에도 불구하고

42 open complicity : 공공연한 공모(共謀)

43 understanding : 합의, 협정, 협약 *cf.* MOU : memorandum of understanding. 양해각서

44   the affair : =the love affair. 연애 사건, 정사(情事)

She dealt with moral problems as a cleaver deals with meat: and in this case she had made up her mind.

It was a bright Sunday morning of early summer, promising heat,[45] but with a fresh breeze blowing. All the windows of the boarding house were open and the lace curtains ballooned gently towards the street beneath the raised sashes.[46] The belfry[47] of George's Church sent out constant peals and worshippers, singly or in groups, traversed the little circus[48] before the church, revealing their purpose by their self-contained[49] demeanour no less than by the little volumes[50] in their gloved hands. Breakfast was over in the boarding house and the table of the breakfast-room was covered with plates on which lay yellow streaks of eggs[51] with morsels of bacon-fat and bacon-rind. Mrs. Mooney sat in the straw arm-chair and watched the servant Mary remove the breakfast things. She

---

45 promising heat : 더워질 것 같은

46 raised sash : 올려진 창틀

47 belfry : =bell tower. 종루(鍾樓), 종탑

48 circus : (여러 도로가 만나는) 광장

49 self-contained : 차분하고 침착한

50 no less than by the little volumes : 작은 책자 못지않게 ＊여기서 '책자'는 기도서(the prayer books)를 가리킴.

51 yellow streaks of eggs : 달걀 노른자 자국들

made Mary collect the crusts and pieces of broken bread to help to make Tuesday's bread-pudding. When the table was cleared, the broken bread collected, the sugar and butter safe under lock and key,[52] she began to reconstruct the interview which she had had the night before with Polly. Things were as she had suspected: she had been frank in her questions and Polly had been frank in her answers. Both had been somewhat awkward, of course. She had been made awkward by her not wishing to receive the news in too cavalier a fashion[53] or to seem to have connived and Polly had been made awkward not merely because allusions of that kind[54] always made her awkward but also because she did not wish it to be thought that in her wise innocence[55] she had divined[56] the intention behind her mother's tolerance.

Mrs. Mooney glanced instinctively at the little gilt clock on the mantelpiece as soon as she had become aware through her revery that the bells of George's Church had stopped ringing.

---

52 safe under lock and key : 자물쇠로 단단히 잠가 둔
53 to receive the news in too cavalier a fashion : 그 소식을 너무 대범하게 받아들이다
54 allusions of that kind : (두 사람의) 연애에 관한 언급
55 in her wise innocence : 영리하게 순진한 척하면서
56 divine : 점치다, 미리 알다

It was seventeen minutes past eleven: she would have lots of time to have the matter out with[57] Mr. Doran and then catch short twelve[58] at Marlborough Street. She was sure she would win. To begin with she had all the weight of social opinion on her side: she was an outraged[59] mother. She had allowed him to live beneath her roof, assuming that he was a man of honour and he had simply abused her hospitality. He was thirty-four or thirty-five years of age, so that youth could not be pleaded as his excuse;[60] nor could ignorance be his excuse since he was a man who had seen something of the world.[61] He had simply taken advantage of Polly's youth and inexperience: that was evident. The question was: What reparation would he make?

There must be reparation made in such case. It is all very well for the man: he can go his ways as if nothing had

---

57 have the matter out with : ~와 토의하여 문제를 해결하다
58 short twelve : <가톨릭> 열두시에 드리는 평미사, 약식 미사 *장엄 미사 (High Mass)와 구별하여 Low Mass라고도 하며 성가대의 합창이나 음악이 따르지 않는 간소한 미사를 가리킴.
59 outrage : (여자를) 범하다, 능욕하다
60 youth could not be pleaded as his excuse : 젊다는 것이 핑곗거리가 될 수 는 없었다
61 see something of the world : 세상(물정)을 조금 알다

happened, having had his moment of pleasure, but the girl has to bear the brunt.[62] Some mothers would be content to patch up[63] such an affair for a sum of money; she had known cases of it. But she would not do so. For her only one reparation could make up for the loss of her daughter's honour: marriage.

She counted all her cards[64] again before sending Mary up to Doran's room to say that she wished to speak with him. She felt sure she would win. He was a serious young man, not rakish[65] or loud-voiced like the others. If it had been Mr. Sheridan or Mr. Meade or Bantam Lyons her task would have been much harder. She did not think he would face publicity.[66] All the lodgers in the house knew something of the affair; details had been invented by some. Besides, he had been employed for thirteen years in a great Catholic wine-merchant's office and publicity would mean for him, perhaps, the loss of his job. Whereas if he agreed all might be well. She

---

62 bear the brunt : 비난을 감수하다 *brunt : (공격의) 예봉, 주력
63 patch up : 임시변통으로 만들다, 대충 고치다
64 card : (결정적인) 방법, 수단
65 rakish : =dissipated. 방탕한
66 face publicity : 세상에 알려지는 것을 받아들이다(견디다)

knew he had a good screw[67] for one thing[68] and she suspected he had a bit of stuff put by.[69]

Nearly the half-hour! She stood up and surveyed herself in the pier-glass.[70] The decisive expression of her great florid face satisfied her and she thought of some mothers she knew who could not get their daughters off their hands.[71]

Mr. Doran was very anxious indeed this Sunday morning. He had made two attempts to shave but his hand had been so unsteady that he had been obliged to desist.[72] Three days' reddish beard fringed his jaws[73] and every two or three minutes a mist gathered on his glasses so that he had to take them off and polish them with his pocket-handkerchief. The recollection of his confession of the night before was a cause of acute pain[74] to him; the priest had drawn out[75] every

---

67 screw : <속어> =salary

68 for one thing : 우선, 무엇보다도

69 had a bit of stuff put by : 약간의 돈을 저축해 놓았다 * put by : =save

70 pier-glass : 체경

71 get their daughters off their hands : 딸을 치우다(결혼시키다)

72 desist : <문어> 그만두다, 단념하다

73 Three days' reddish beard fringed his jaws : 사흘 동안 깎지 못한 불그레한 턱수염이 턱 둘레를 에워쌌다

74 acute pain : 급성 통증

75 draw out : 끌어내다, 캐내다

ridiculous detail of the affair and in the end had so magnified his sin that he was almost thankful at being afforded a loophole of reparation.[76] The harm was done. What could he do now but marry her or run away? He could not brazen it out.[77] The affair would be sure to be talked of and his employer would be certain to hear of it. Dublin is such a small city: everyone knows everyone else's business. He felt his heart leap warmly in his throat as he heard in his excited imagination old Mr. Leonard calling out in his rasping voice:[78] "Send Mr. Doran here, please."

All his long years of service gone for nothing![79] All his industry and diligence thrown away![80] As a young man he had sown his wild oats,[81] of course; he had boasted of his freethinking and denied the existence of God to his companions in public-houses. But that was all passed and done with... nearly. He still bought a copy of *Reynolds's Newspaper* every

---

76 a loophole of reparation : 속죄(보상)의 길
77 brazen it out : 뻔뻔스럽게 밀고 나가다, 끝까지 딱 잡아떼다
78 in his rasping voice : 귀에 거슬리는(불안하게 만드는) 목소리로
79 go for nothing : =be without reward or result
80 throw away : =waste. 허비하다
81 sow one's wild oats : 젊어서 난봉피우다

week but he attended to his religious duties[82] and for nine-tenths of the year lived a regular life. He had money enough to settle down on;[83] it was not that. But the family would look down on her. First of all there was her disreputable father and then her mother's boarding house was beginning to get a certain fame.[84] He had a notion that he was being had.[85] He could imagine his friends talking of the affair and laughing. She was a little vulgar; some times she said "I seen" and "If I had've known." But what would grammar matter if he really loved her? He could not make up his mind whether to like her or despise her for what she had done. Of course he had done it too. His instinct urged him to remain free, not to marry. Once you are married you are done for,[86] it said.

While he was sitting helplessly on the side of the bed in shirt and trousers she tapped lightly at his door and entered.

---

82 religious duty: 종교적 직무 *duty: (교회의) 종무(宗務), 예배식의 근행(勤行)

83 settle down on: (결혼하여) 자리를 잡다

84 get a certain fame: 이름을 내다, (특히) 악명을 떨치다 *앞서 말한 '떠돌이 예술가'들이 들락날락하는 이상한 하숙집으로 소문이 나고 있음을 가리킴.

85 have: =deceive, cheat. 속이다, 기만하다

86 you are done for: 넌 끝장이다 *do for: 죽이다, 망하게 하다

She told him all, that she had made a clean breast of[87] it to her mother and that her mother would speak with him that morning. She cried and threw her arms round his neck, saying:

"O Bob! Bob! What am I to do? What am I to do at all?"

She would put an end to[88] herself, she said.

He comforted her feebly, telling her not to cry, that it would be all right, never fear. He felt against his shirt the agitation of her bosom.

It was not altogether his fault that it had happened. He remembered well, with the curious patient memory of the celibate,[89] the first casual caresses her dress, her breath, her fingers had given him. Then late one night as he was undressing for bed she had tapped at his door, timidly. She wanted to relight her candle at his for hers had been blown out by a gust. It was her bath night. She wore a loose open

---

87 make a clean breast of: =confess. (비밀, 죄 등을) 터놓고 말하다, 낱낱이 고백하다

88 put an end to: =kill

89 with the curious patient memory of the celibate: 독신자 특유의 호기심 많고 끈기 있는 기억력으로

combing-jacket of printed flannel.[90] Her white instep[91] shone in the opening of her furry slippers and the blood[92] glowed warmly behind her perfumed skin. From her hands and wrists too as she lit and steadied her candle a faint perfume arose.

On nights when he came in very late it was she who warmed up his dinner. He scarcely knew what he was eating feeling her beside him alone, at night, in the sleeping house.[93] And her thoughtfulness! If the night was anyway cold or wet or windy there was sure to be a little tumbler of punch[94] ready for him. Perhaps they could be happy together....

They used to go upstairs together on tiptoe,[95] each with a candle, and on the third landing exchange reluctant goodnights. They used to kiss. He remembered well her eyes, the touch of her hand and his delirium....[96]

But delirium passes. He echoed[97] her phrase, applying it

---

90 combing-jacket of printed flannel : 무늬를 넣은 플란넬 화장복

91 instep : 발등

92 the blood : 혈색

93 in the sleeping house : 모두가 잠든 집에서

94 a little tumbler of punch : 펀치 한 잔

95 on tiptoe : 까치발로, 살금살금

96 delirium : =wild excitement. 황홀감

97 echo : 흉내 내다, 되풀이하다

to himself: "What am I to do?" The instinct of the celibate warned him to hold back. But the sin was there; even his sense of honour told him that reparation must be made for such a sin.

While he was sitting with her on the side of the bed Mary ₅ came to the door and said that the missus wanted to see him in the parlour. He stood up to put on his coat and waistcoat, more helpless than ever. When he was dressed he went over to her to comfort her. It would be all right, never fear. He left her crying on the bed and moaning softly: "O my God!" ₁₀

Going down the stairs his glasses became so dimmed with moisture that he had to take them off and polish them. He longed to ascend through the roof and fly away to another country where he would never hear again of his trouble, and yet a force pushed him downstairs step by step. The ₁₅ implacable[98] faces of his employer and of the Madam stared upon his discomfiture.[99] On the last flight[100] of stairs he passed Jack Mooney who was coming up from the pantry[101]

---

98 implacable : =relentless. 무자비한, 사정없는
99 discomfiture : =embarrassment, confusion. 당황, 당혹, 낭패
100 the last flight : 마지막 계단 * flight : (층계참과 층계참 사이의) 계단
101 pantry : (부엌 또는 식당에 인접한) 식료품 저장실

nursing[102] two bottles of *Bass*.[103] They saluted coldly; and the lover's eyes rested for a second or two on a thick bulldog face and a pair of thick short arms. When he reached the foot of the staircase he glanced up and saw Jack regarding him from the door of the return-room.[104]

Suddenly he remembered the night when one of the music-hall artistes, a little blond Londoner, had made a rather free[105] allusion to Polly. The reunion had been almost broken up on account of Jack's violence. Everyone tried to quiet him. The music-hall artiste, a little paler than usual, kept smiling and saying that there was no harm meant: but Jack kept shouting at him that if any fellow tried that sort of a game on with his sister he'd bloody well put his teeth down his throat,[106] so he would.[107]

Polly sat for a little time on the side of the bed, crying. Then she dried her eyes and went over to the looking-glass. She

---

102 nurse : =clasp caressingly. 껴안다, 부둥켜안다

103 *Bass* : 배스 맥주

104 return-room : 모퉁이 방

105 free : 지나친, 절도 없는, 방자한, 추잡한

106 he'd bloody well put his teeth down his throat : 이를 확실하게 목구멍 속으로 처박아 버리겠다고

107 so he would : =really he would do so. 정말 그렇게 할 인간이었다

dipped the end of the towel in the water-jug and refreshed her eyes with the cool water. She looked at herself in profile and readjusted a hairpin above her ear. Then she went back to the bed again and sat at the foot. She regarded the pillows for a long time and the sight of them awakened in her mind secret, amiable memories. She rested the nape of her neck against the cool iron bed-rail and fell into a reverie. There was no longer any perturbation[108] visible on her face.

She waited on patiently, almost cheerfully, without alarm, her memories gradually giving place to[109] hopes and visions of the future. Her hopes and visions were so intricate[110] that she no longer saw the white pillows on which her gaze was fixed or remembered that she was waiting for anything.

At last she heard her mother calling. She started to her feet and ran to the banisters.

"Polly! Polly!"

"Yes, mamma?"

"Come down, dear. Mr. Doran wants to speak to you."

Then she remembered what she had been waiting for.

---

108 perturbation : 불안감, 동요
109 give place to : =be succeeded by. 자리를 내어 주다, 이어지다
110 intricate : =complicated

작품 해설

1. Mr. Doran's dilemma

포도주 도매상에 근무하는 30대 중반의 건실한 청년 Mr. Doran은 원치 않는 결혼을 해야 하는 곤경에 처해 있다. 하숙집 주인 딸 Polly와 약간의 로맨스가 있었는데 어느 순간 정신을 차려 보니 그녀와 결혼할 수밖에 없는 끔찍한 상황에 처해 있는 것이다. 문제는 자신이 정말로 그녀와 사랑에 빠진 것도 아니며, 더욱이 그녀가 결혼해도 괜찮을 만큼 좋은 여자가 아니라는 것을 스스로 잘 알고 있다는 점이다. 직감적으로 "당했다"(he was being had)는 느낌마저 든다. 내면의 목소리는 그녀와 결혼하면 안 된다고 말하지만, 그는 결국 그 결혼을 받아들이게 되리라는 것을 알고 있다. 결혼을 거부하기에는 주위의 이목과 세상의 평판이 너무 두렵고, 상황은 자신이 죗값(?)을 치러야 한다는 쪽으로 돌아가고 있는 것이다. 심지어 고해성사를 하러 간 신부에게서조차 그는 아무런 위로를 받지 못한다. 마치 올가미에 걸린 듯 꼼짝달싹 못 하는 심약한 청년의 절망감이 짙게 배어나는 우울한 단편이다.

"The Boarding House"의 어두운 분위기는 맥락을 살펴보고 나면 한결 이해가 쉬워진다. 이 작품은 James Joyce의 단편소설집 *Dubliners*에 수록된 15편 중의 하나로, 작가는 이 작품집을 관통하는 키워드를

'마비'(paralysis)라는 한 단어로 요약한 바 있다. 20세기 초 아일랜드의 수도 더블린 시민들의 암울한 풍경을 묘사하면서 작가는 '마비'라는 단어를 떠올린 것이다. 이 단편집의 주인공들은 예외 없이 일종의 마비 양상을 보이며, Mr. Doran의 의식과 행동 역시 마비된 인물의 전형적 징후에 해당한다. "나 어떡해요?"(what am I to do?)라는 Polly의 교활한 질문은 고스란히 Doran이 처한 절망적 상황에 해당한다. 상대방이 도저히 빠져나갈 수 없는 올가미를 마련한 Mrs. Mooney는 여유 있게 Doran을 기다리고 있고, 아래층으로 소환된 Doran은 지붕을 뚫고 날아올라 어디 먼 나라로 달아나고 싶은 심경이다. 하지만 의지와 달리 그의 두 발은 마치 마비라도 된 듯 한 걸음씩 계단을 내려가고 있을 뿐이다.

2. Mother and daughter

'마비'라는 키워드에 주목한다면 유감스럽게도 이 작품의 주인공은 Mr. Doran이라기보다 Mrs. Mooney와 그녀의 딸 Polly라고 해야 옳다. 엄밀히 말해 그들은 Doran보다 더 심각한 마비의 징후를 보이기 때문이다. Doran은 그나마 자신이 지켜야 할 명예와 탈출해야 할 절망적 상황에 대한 이해와 고뇌가 있다. 하지만 모녀는 그와 다르다. 한 인간을 죽음과도 같은 늪에 빠뜨려 놓았지만 그들은 자신이 무엇을 잘못했는지 깨닫지 못하고 있다. 청년을 사지로 몰아넣기 위해 두 사람은 '공모 아닌 공모'를 해 놓고도 서로 모른 척 시치미를 뗄 뿐, 그들에게는 그저 마비된 양심만 있을 뿐이다.

Mrs. Mooney의 관심은 오로지 Doran의 월급과 저축해 놓은 돈에 있으며, 따라서 결혼문제는 돈 거래거나 아니면 반드시 이겨야 할 싸움이 되어 버렸다. 은밀하게 기다린 끝에 그녀는 결정적 시점을 포착하였고, 자신이 그 싸움에서 이길 것을 확신한다("She was sure she would win.") 요컨대 작품의 기본 소재는 사랑과 결혼이지만 애틋한 로맨스의 결실로 이루어지는 숭고한 결혼에 대한 인식은 그들에게서 전혀 찾아볼 수 없다. 작품 초입에 주정뱅이 남편과의 결혼을 별거로 마무리한 Mrs. Mooney의 파탄난 결혼생활에서 이들의 메마른 정서와 마비된 의식은 이미 예고된 바 있다. 더욱이 Mrs. Mooney를 가리키는 호칭 "the Madam"이 때로는 사창가의 포주를 의미한다는 점에서 서술자는 Mrs. Mooney가 딸을 "팔아넘긴" 것으로 해석해도 무방하다는 암시를 넌지시 던지고 있다고도 볼 수 있다. 신성한 결혼은 어디에도 없다.

3. 절제된 서사

짧은 단편이지만 스토리는 Mrs. Mooney와 Mr. Doran이 대면하는 결정적 순간을 향해 조금씩 다가가고, 긴장은 점점 더 고조되고 있다. 계단에서 만난 Polly의 오빠 Jack의 존재는 Doran에게 거의 협박으로 다가온다. 하지만 두 사람이 대면하는 결정적 순간에 서술자는 슬쩍 시선을 돌린다. 마치 영화의 한 장면처럼 화면은 이층 Doran의 침실에 남아 있는 Polly에게 넘어가는 것이다. 그리고 잠시 후 아래층에서 Mrs. Mooney의 목소리가 들려온다.

"Polly! Polly!"
"Yes, mamma?"

"Come down, dear. Mr. Doran wants to speak to you."

마치 푸줏간 주인이 고기를 자르듯이 Mrs. Mooney는 한칼에 문제를 해결하고 Polly를 부르는 것이다. 상황 종료. 서술자는 모친과 청년이 마주한 결정적 순간의 기록을 텍스트의 빈 공간 속에 집어넣고 예의 무덤덤한 어조로 서사를 마무리한다. 작가는 언어와 감정을 절제하는 완곡한 표현과 서술로 Doran의 아득한 체념과 절망을 재현하는 데 성공하였다. 이제 빈 공간을 채우는 것은 독자들의 상상력이고, 이를 촉발시킨 것은 전지적 작가(the omniscient author)의 놀라운 자제력이다.

영미 명작 단편선_8

The Rocking-Horse Winner

D. H. Lawrence

D. H. Lawrence(1885~1930)는 20세기 초반에 활동한 영국 소설가로 *Sons and Lovers*(1913), *Women in Love*(1920) 등의 대표작이 있으며, 단편소설이나 시, 비평 등에서도 수준 높은 작품을 많이 남겼다. "The Rocking-Horse Winner"(1926)는 아들과 어머니 사이에 벌어지는 기이한 애착의 문제를 다루고 있다는 점에서 이른바 오이디푸스 콤플렉스(Oedipus complex)와 관련이 있는데, 모자간의 왜곡된 관계 형성의 배경에는 서구 문명의 핵심과제인 자본주의적 물신숭배의 문제가 깔려 있다. Lawrence는 근대 이후 서구문명의 문제는 구체적으로 왜곡된 남녀관계의 전개로 나타난다고 보았고, 이 작품에서는 특히 설화적 환상성을 도입하여 더욱 신비롭고 설득력 있는 이야기로 발전시키고 있다.

The Rocking-Horse Winner

There was a woman who was beautiful, who started with all the advantages, yet she had no luck. She married for love,[1] and the love turned to dust.[2] She had bonny[3] children, yet she felt they had been thrust upon her,[4] and she could not love them. They looked at her coldly, as if they were finding fault with her. And hurriedly she felt she must cover up[5] some fault in herself. Yet what it was that she must cover up she never knew. Nevertheless, when her children were present, she always felt the centre of her heart go hard.[6] This troubled her, and in her manner she was all the more gentle and anxious for

---

1 marry for love: 사랑을 하여 결혼을 하다
2 turn to dust: 사라지다, 허사가 되다
3 bonny: 귀여운, 어여쁜
4 she felt they had been thrust upon her: 그녀는 아이들을 떠맡았다는 느낌이 들었다
5 cover up: 가리다, 은폐하다
6 hard: 딱딱하게 굳은, 냉정한, 매정한

her children, as if she loved them very much. Only she herself knew that at the centre of her heart was a hard little place that could not feel love, no, not for anybody. Everybody else said of her: "She is such a good mother. She adores her children." Only she herself, and her children themselves, knew it was not so. They read it in each other's eyes.

There were a boy and two little girls. They lived in a pleasant house, with a garden, and they had discreet[7] servants, and felt themselves superior to anyone in the neighbourhood.

Although they lived in style,[8] they felt always an anxiety in the house. There was never enough money. The mother had a small income, and the father had a small income, but not nearly enough for the social position which they had to keep up.[9] The father went into town[10] to some office. But though

---

7 discreet: 신중한, 조심스러운

8 live in style: 호화롭게(품위 있게) 살다 *style: =an elegant, fashionable, or luxurious mode of living. 우아함, 품격

9 the social position which they had to keep up: 그들이 유지해야 하는 사회적 지위

10 town: <런던 인근 지역에서> 런던 *원래는 대문자를 써서 Town으로 런던을 나타냄.

he had good prospects,[11] these prospects never materialised.[12] There was always the grinding[13] sense of the shortage of money, though the style was always kept up.

At last the mother said: "I will see if I can't make something." But she did not know where to begin. She racked her brains,[14] and tried this thing and the other, but could not find anything successful. The failure made deep lines[15] come into her face. Her children were growing up, they would have to go to school.[16] There must be more money, there must be more money. The father, who was always very handsome and expensive in his tastes,[17] seemed as if he never *would* be able to do anything worth doing.[18] And the mother, who had a great belief in herself, did not succeed any better, and her tastes were just as expensive.

---

11 have good prospects : 전망이 좋다

12 materialise : =become actual or real

13 grinding : 끝도 없이 계속되는

14 rack one's brains : 머리를 짜내다, 깊이 생각하다

15 lines : 주름살

16 would have to go to school : 곧 학교를 가야 했다

17 expensive in his tastes : 값비싼 것에 취향이 있는

18 seemed as if he never *would* be able to do anything worth doing : 가치 있는 어떤 일을 해낼 수 없을 것처럼 보였다

And so the house came to be haunted[19] by the unspoken phrase: *There must be more money! There must be more money!* The children could hear it all the time though nobody said it aloud. They heard it at Christmas, when the expensive and splendid toys filled the nursery. Behind the shining modern rocking-horse,[20] behind the smart[21] doll's house, a voice would start whispering: "There *must* be more money! There *must* be more money!" And the children would stop playing, to listen for a moment. They would look into each other's eyes, to see if they had all heard. And each one saw in the eyes of the other two that they too had heard. "There *must* be more money! There *must* be more money!"

It came whispering from the springs of the still-swaying[22] rocking-horse, and even the horse, bending his wooden, champing[23] head, heard it. The big doll, sitting so pink and smirking[24] in her new pram, could hear it quite plainly, and seemed to be smirking all the more self-consciously because

---

19 haunt : (유령이) 출몰하다, (걱정, 고민이) 괴롭히다
20 rocking-horse : (유아용) 흔들목마
21 smart : 말쑥한, 산뜻한, 고급의
22 still-swaying : 계속해서 흔들거리는
23 champ : (말이) 재갈을 신경질적으로 씹다, 여물을 우적우적 씹다
24 smirk : 능글맞게 웃다, 부자연스러운 웃음을 웃다

of it. The foolish puppy, too, that took the place of the teddy-bear, he was looking so extraordinarily foolish for no other reason but that he heard the secret whisper all over the house: "There *must* be more money!"

Yet nobody ever said it aloud. The whisper was everywhere, and therefore no one spoke it. Just as no one ever says: "We are breathing!" in spite of the fact that breath is coming and going all the time.

"Mother," said the boy Paul one day, "why don't we keep a car of our own? Why do we always use uncle's, or else a taxi?"

"Because we're the poor members of the family," said the mother.

"But why *are* we, mother?"

"Well—I suppose," she said slowly and bitterly, "it's because your father has no luck."

The boy was silent for some time.

"Is luck money, mother?" he asked, rather timidly.

"No, Paul. Not quite.[25] It's what causes you to have money."

"Oh!" said Paul vaguely. "I thought when Uncle Oscar said *filthy lucker*, it meant money."

---

25 Not quite : =Not exactly

"*Filthy lucre*[26] does mean money," said the mother. "But it's lucre, not luck."

"Oh!" said the boy. "Then what is luck, mother?"

"It's what causes you to have money. If you're lucky you have money. That's why it's better to be born lucky than rich. If you're rich, you may lose your money. But if you're lucky, you will always get more money."

"Oh! Will you? And is father not lucky?"

"Very unlucky, I should say,"[27] she said bitterly.

The boy watched her with unsure[28] eyes.

"Why?" he asked.

"I don't know. Nobody ever knows why one person is lucky and another unlucky."

"Don't they? Nobody at all? Does *nobody* know?"

"Perhaps God. But He never tells."

"He ought to, then. And aren't you lucky either, mother?"

"I can't be, if I married an unlucky husband."

"But by yourself,[29] aren't you?"

---

26 filthy lucre : 부정 이득 ＊lucre : 이익, 이득
27 Very unlucky, I should say : 아마 매우 운이 없다고 해야겠지
28 unsure : 확신이 없는
29 by yourself : 어머니 혼자는요

"I used to think I was, before I married. Now I think I am very unlucky indeed."

"Why?"

"Well — never mind! Perhaps I'm not really,"[30] she said.

The child looked at her to see if she meant it.[31] But he saw, by the lines of her mouth, that she was only trying to hide something from him.

"Well, anyhow," he said stoutly, "I'm a lucky person."

"Why?" said his mother, with a sudden laugh.

He stared at her. He didn't even know why he had said it.

"God told me," he asserted, brazening it out.[32]

"I hope He did, dear!" she said, again with a laugh, but rather bitter.

"He did, mother!"

"Excellent!" said the mother, using one of her husband's exclamations.

The boy saw she did not believe him; or rather, that she paid no attention to his assertion. This angered him somewhat, and made him want to compel her attention.

---

30 I'm not really : =I'm not really lucky
31 if she meant it : 어머니의 말이 진심인지
32 brazen it out : 태연하게(뻔뻔하게) 행동하다

He went off[33] by himself, vaguely, in a childish way, seeking for the clue to "luck". Absorbed, taking no heed of other people, he went about[34] with a sort of stealth,[35] seeking inwardly for luck. He wanted luck, he wanted it, he wanted it. When the two girls were playing dolls in the nursery, he would sit on his big rocking-horse, charging[36] madly into space, with a frenzy[37] that made the little girls peer at him uneasily. Wildly the horse careered,[38] the waving dark hair of the boy tossed, his eyes had a strange glare in them. The little girls dared not speak to him.

When he had ridden to the end of his mad little journey, he climbed down and stood in front of his rocking-horse, staring fixedly into its lowered face. Its red mouth was slightly open, its big eye was wide and glassy-bright.

"Now!" he would silently command the snorting steed.[39] "Now, take me to where there is luck! Now take me!"

---

33 go off : (특히 무엇을 하러) 자리를 뜨다
34 go about : 이리저리 돌아다니다
35 with a sort of stealth : 약간 은밀하게
36 charge : (적을 향하여) 공격하다, 돌격하다
37 with a frenzy : 광분하여
38 career : 질주하다, 무턱대고 달리다
39 the snorting steed : 힝힝거리는 말

And he would slash the horse on the neck with the little whip he had asked Uncle Oscar for. He *knew* the horse could take him to where there was luck, if only he forced it. So he would mount again and start on his furious ride, hoping at last to get there. He knew he could get there.

"You'll break your horse, Paul!" said the nurse.

"He's always riding like that! I wish he'd leave off!"[40] said his elder sister Joan.

But he only glared[41] down on them in silence. Nurse gave him up. She could make nothing of[42] him. Anyhow,[43] he was growing beyond her.

One day his mother and his Uncle Oscar came in when he was on one of his furious rides. He did not speak to them.

"Hallo, you young jockey![44] Riding a winner?"[45] said his uncle.

"Aren't you growing too big for a rocking-horse? You're not a very little boy any longer, you know," said his mother.

---

40 leave off: 중단하다, 멈추다

41 glare: 노려보다

42 make nothing of: ~을 이해할 수 없다

43 anyhow: 어쨌든, 여하튼

44 jockey: (경마에서 특히 직업적으로 말을 타는) 기수

45 a winner: 우승마

But Paul only gave a blue glare from his big, rather close-set eyes.[46] He would speak to nobody when he was in full tilt.[47] His mother watched him with an anxious expression on her face.

At last he suddenly stopped forcing his horse into the mechanical gallop and slid down.

"Well, I got there!" he announced fiercely, his blue eyes still flaring, and his sturdy long legs straddling[48] apart.

"Where did you get to?" asked his mother.

"Where I wanted to go," he flared[49] back at her.

"That's right, son!" said Uncle Oscar. "Don't you stop[50] till you get there. What's the horse's name?"

"He doesn't have a name," said the boy.

"Gets on[51] without[52] all right?" asked the uncle.

---

46 close-set eyes : 모들뜨기 눈(두 눈동자가 안쪽으로 치우친 눈을 가리킴)
  * close-set : 한 데로 몰린, 밀집된
47 in full tilt : =in full speed
48 straddle : 다리를 벌리고 서다(앉다)
49 flare : 버럭 화를 내다, 소리를 지르다
50 Don't you stop : =Don't stop
51 get on : (사회 생활 등에서) 성공하다
52 without : =without a name

"Well, he has different names. He was called Sansovino[53] last week."

"Sansovino, eh? Won the Ascot.[54] How did you know this name?"

"He always talks about horse-races with Bassett," said Joan.

The uncle was delighted to find that his small nephew was posted[55] with all the racing news. Bassett, the young gardener, who had been wounded in the left foot in the war and had got his present job through Oscar Cresswell, whose batman[56] he had been, was a perfect blade[57] of the "turf".[58] He lived in the racing events,[59] and the small boy lived with him.

Oscar Cresswell got it all from Bassett.

"Master Paul[60] comes and asks me, so I can't do more than

---

53 Sansovino : (원래는) 이탈리아 르네상스 시대의 조각가, 건축가

54 Won the Ascot : 애스컷에서 우승했지 *the Ascot : 애스컷 경마장. 런던 서쪽 40km 거리에 있는 경마장으로 매년 6월 셋째 주에 화려하고 유서 깊은 애스컷 경마대회가 열림.

55 posted : <구어> 사정에 밝은 *well-posted : 정통한

56 batman : <영국, 군사> (육군 장교의) 당번병

57 blade : <드물게> (경마 등에서) 기세 있는(빼기는) 청년

58 the "turf" : 경마장, 경마계 *turf : 잔디, 뗏장

59 live in the racing events : 경마에 빠져 살다

60 Master Paul : 폴 도련님 *'master'는 하인이 주인집 어린 아이를 부르는 호칭.

tell him, sir," said Bassett, his face terribly serious, as if he were speaking of religious matters.

"And does he ever put anything on[61] a horse he fancies?"[62]

"Well — I don't want to give him away[63] — he's a young sport,[64] a fine sport, sir. Would you mind asking him himself? He sort of takes a pleasure in it, and perhaps he'd feel I was giving him away, sir, if you don't mind."

Bassett was serious as a church.[65]

The uncle went back to his nephew and took him off for a ride in the car.

"Say, Paul, old man,[66] do you ever put anything on a horse?" the uncle asked.

The boy watched the handsome man closely.

"Why, do you think I oughtn't to?" he parried.[67]

"Not a bit of it! I thought perhaps you might give me a tip

---

61 put on : (경마 등에서) 돈을 걸다
62 fancy : (특히 경마에서) 우승 후보로 여기다
63 give him away : 그의 비밀을 누설하다
64 sport : <구어> 노름꾼, 도박꾼
65 serious as a church : 무척 심각한(진지한)
66 old man : =old boy, old chap. 어이, 친구 *중년 이상의 나이 지긋한 남자
    들끼리의 친근한 호칭.
67 parry : (공격이나 질문 등을) 슬쩍 피하다, 받아넘기다, 얼버무리다

for the Lincoln."[68]

The car sped on into the country, going down to Uncle Oscar's place[69] in Hampshire.[70]

"Honour bright?"[71] said the nephew.

"Honour bright, son!" said the uncle.

"Well, then, Daffodil."

"Daffodil! I doubt it, sonny.[72] What about Mirza?"[73]

"I only know the winner," said the boy. "That's Daffodil."

"Daffodil, eh?"

There was a pause. Daffodil was an obscure horse comparatively.

"Uncle!"

"Yes, son?"

"You won't let it go any further,[74] will you? I promised Bassett."

---

68 the Lincoln: 링컨 (경마)대회

69 place: =house, home

70 Hampshire: 영국 잉글랜드 남부의 주 ＊런던에서 서남쪽으로 한 시간 거리에 있음.

71 honour bright: =upon my honour, really and truly. 맹세코, 틀림없이

72 sonny: 얘야, 자네, 젊은이

73 mirza: (페르시아, 이란에서) 왕자(royal prince)

74 won't let it go any further: 더 이상 퍼져나가지 않게 하다

"Bassett be damned,[75] old man! What's he got to do with it?"

"We're partners. We've been partners from the first. Uncle, he lent me my first five shillings, which I lost. I promised him, honour bright, it was only between me and him; only you gave me that ten-shilling note I started winning with, so I thought 5 you were lucky. You won't let it go any further, will you?"

The boy gazed at his uncle from those big, hot, blue eyes, set rather close together. The uncle stirred[76] and laughed uneasily.

"Right you are, son! I'll keep your tip private. Daffodil, eh? How much are you putting on him?" 10

"All except twenty pounds," said the boy. "I keep that in reserve."[77]

The uncle thought it a good joke.

"You keep twenty pounds in reserve, do you, you young romancer?[78] What are you betting, then?" 15

"I'm betting three hundred," said the boy gravely. "But it's between you and me, Uncle Oscar! Honour bright?"

The uncle burst into a roar of laughter.

---

75 Bassett be damned : =Bassett is not important

76 stir : 분발하다, 흥분하다

77 in reserve : 예비로, 비축금으로

78 romancer : 공상가, 몽상가, 터무니없이 꾸민 말을 하는 사람

"It's between you and me all right, you young Nat Gould,"[79] he said, laughing. "But where's your three hundred?"

"Bassett keeps it for me. We're partners."

"You are, are you! And what is Bassett putting on Daffodil?"

"He won't go quite as high as I do, I expect. Perhaps he'll go a hundred and fifty."

"What, pennies?" laughed the uncle.

"Pounds," said the child, with a surprised look at his uncle. "Bassett keeps a bigger reserve than I do."

Between wonder and amusement Uncle Oscar was silent. He pursued the matter no further, but he determined to take his nephew with him to the Lincoln races.

"Now, son," he said, "I'm putting twenty on Mirza, and I'll put five on for you on any horse you fancy. What's your pick?"[80]

"Daffodil, uncle."

"No, not the fiver[81] on Daffodil!"

"I should if it was my own fiver," said the child.

---

79 Nat Gould : (1857~1919) 영국의 소설가 *경마를 무척 좋아하여 소설의 소재로 경마를 많이 활용하였음.

80 pick : 선택한 것

81 fiver : 5파운드(달러)짜리 지폐

"Good! Good! Right you are! A fiver for me and a fiver for you on Daffodil."

The child had never been to a race-meeting[82] before, and his eyes were blue fire. He pursed his mouth[83] tight and watched. A Frenchman just in front had put his money on Lancelot.[84] Wild with excitement, he flayed[85] his arms up and down, yelling "Lancelot! Lancelot!" in his French accent.

Daffodil came in first, Lancelot second, Mirza third. The child, flushed and with eyes blazing,[86] was curiously serene. His uncle brought him four five-pound notes, four to one.[87]

"What am I to do with these?" he cried, waving them before the boy's eyes.

"I suppose we'll talk to Bassett," said the boy. "I expect I have fifteen hundred now; and twenty in reserve; and this twenty."

---

82 a race-meeting : 경마대회

83 purse one's mouth : 입을 오므리다 ＊보통 purse one's lips로 사용함.

84 Lancelot : 남자 이름 ＊Arthur왕 전설의 원탁의 기사 중 가장 뛰어난 기사로 Guinevere 왕비의 연인이었음.

85 flay : (가죽이 벗겨지도록) 후려치다, (동물의) 가죽을 벗기다 ＊여기서는 흥분해서 팔을 휘두르는 동작을 이렇게 표현한 것임.

86 flushed and with eyes blazing : 얼굴이 시뻘게지고 눈을 이글거리며

87 four to one : 4대 1(네 배)의 배당을 가리킴.

His uncle studied[88] him for some moments.

"Look here, son!" he said. "You're not serious about Bassett and that fifteen hundred, are you?"

"Yes, I am. But it's between you and me, uncle. Honour bright!"

"Honour bright all right, son! But I must talk to Bassett."

"If you'd like to be a partner, uncle, with Bassett and me, we could all be partners. Only, you'd have to promise, honour bright, uncle, not to let it go beyond us three. Bassett and I are lucky, and you must be lucky, because it was your ten shillings I started winning with...."

Uncle Oscar took both Bassett and Paul into Richmond Park[89] for an afternoon, and there they talked.

"It's like this, you see, sir," Bassett said. "Master Paul would get me talking about racing events, spinning yarns,[90] you know, sir. And he was always keen on knowing if I'd made or if I'd lost. It's about a year since,[91] now, that I put five shillings

---

88   study: 찬찬히 살피다, 유심히 바라보다
89   Richmond Park: 런던 서남부에 있는 영국 왕실 공원으로 엄청난 규모를 자랑함.
90   spin a yarn: 황당하고 과장된 이야기를 하다
91   since: =ago

on Blush of Dawn[92] for him — and we lost. Then the luck turned, with that ten shillings he had from you, that we put on Singhalese.[93] And since that time, it's been pretty steady, all things considering.[94] What do you say, Master Paul?"

"We're all right when we're sure," said Paul. "It's when we're not quite sure that we go down."[95]

"Oh, but we're careful then," said Bassett.

"But when are you sure?" smiled Uncle Oscar.

"It's Master Paul, sir," said Bassett in a secret, religious voice. "It's as if he had it from heaven. Like Daffodil, now, for the Lincoln. That was as sure as eggs."[96]

"Did you put anything on Daffodil?" asked Oscar Cresswell.

"Yes, sir. I made my bit."

"And my nephew?"

Bassett was obstinately silent, looking at Paul.

"I made twelve hundred, didn't I, Bassett? I told uncle I was putting three hundred on Daffodil."

---

92 Blush of Dawn : 푸크시아(fuchsia) 꽃의 별칭

93 Singhalese : =Sinhalese. 스리랑카에 사는 한 부족의 이름

94 all things considering : =all things considered

95 go down : 지다, 패하다

96 as sure as eggs : <고어> 분명한, 확실한 cf. One day he'll realize that I was right, as sure as eggs is eggs.

"That's right," said Bassett, nodding.

"But where's the money?" asked the uncle.

"I keep it safe locked up, sir. Master Paul he can have it any minute[97] he likes to ask for it."

"What, fifteen hundred pounds?"

"And twenty! And forty, that is, with the twenty he made on the course."

"It's amazing!" said the uncle.

"If Master Paul offers you to be partners, sir, I would, if I were you; if you'll excuse me," said Bassett.

Oscar Cresswell thought about it.

"I'll see the money," he said.

They drove home again, and sure enough,[98] Bassett came round to the garden-house with fifteen hundred pounds in notes. The twenty pounds reserve was left with Joe Glee, in the Turf Commission deposit.[99]

"You see, it's all right, uncle, when I'm sure! Then we go strong, for all we're worth,[100] don't we, Bassett?"

---

97 any minute : =soon, imminently

98 sure enough : =actually

99 the Turf Commission deposit : 경마 수수료 예치금

100 for all one is worth : <비격식> =to the utmost

"We do that, Master Paul."

"And when are you sure?" said the uncle, laughing.

"Oh, well, sometimes I'm absolutely sure, like about Daffodil," said the boy; "and sometimes I have an idea; and sometimes I haven't even an idea, have I, Bassett? Then we're careful, because we mostly go down."

"You do, do you! And when you're sure, like about Daffodil, what makes you sure, sonny?"

"Oh, well, I don't know," said the boy uneasily. "I'm sure, you know, uncle; that's all."

"It's as if he had it from heaven, sir," Bassett reiterated.

"I should say so!" said the uncle.

But he became a partner. And when the Leger[101] was coming on, Paul was "sure" about Lively Spark, which was a quite inconsiderable horse. The boy insisted on putting a thousand on the horse, Bassett went for five hundred, and Oscar Cresswell two hundred. Lively Spark came in first, and the betting had been ten to one against him. Paul had made ten thousand.

"You see," he said. "I was absolutely sure of him."

---

101 the Leger : =St Leger Stakes *Doncaster에서 열리는 경마대회로 영국의 5대 classic race 중의 하나임.

Even Oscar Cresswell had cleared[102] two thousand.

"Look here, son," he said, "this sort of thing makes me nervous."

"It needn't, uncle! Perhaps I shan't be sure again for a long time."

"But what are you going to do with your money?" asked the uncle.

"Of course," said the boy, "I started it for mother. She said she had no luck, because father is unlucky, so I thought if I was lucky, it might stop whispering."

"What might stop whispering?"

"Our house. I hate our house for whispering."

"What does it whisper?"

"Why — why" — the boy fidgeted[103] — "why, I don't know. But it's always short of money, you know, uncle."

"I know it, son, I know it."

"You know people send mother writs,[104] don't you, uncle?"

"I'm afraid I do," said the uncle.

"And then the house whispers, like people laughing at you

---

102 clear : 수익을 올리다

103 fidget : 안절부절못하다, 초조해하다

104 writ : 영장, 집행명령, 서류

behind your back. It's awful, that is! I thought if I was lucky...."

"You might stop it," added the uncle.

The boy watched him with big blue eyes, that had an uncanny[105] cold fire in them, and he said never a word.

"Well, then!" said the uncle. "What are we doing?"   5

"I shouldn't like mother to know I was lucky," said the boy.

"Why not, son?"

"She'd stop me."

"I don't think she would."

"Oh!" — and the boy writhed in an odd way — "I don't want   10
her to know, uncle."

"All right, son! We'll manage it without her knowing."

They managed it very easily. Paul, at the other's suggestion, handed over five thousand pounds to his uncle, who deposited it with the family lawyer,[106] who was then to inform Paul's   15
mother that a relative had put five thousand pounds into his
hands, which sum was to be paid out a thousand pounds at a
time, on the mother's birthday, for the next five years.

"So she'll have a birthday present of a thousand pounds for
five successive years," said Uncle Oscar. "I hope it won't make   20

---

105 uncanny: 기괴한, 신비스러운
106 deposit A with B: A를 B에게 맡기다

it all the harder for her later."

Paul's mother had her birthday in November. The house had been "whispering" worse than ever lately, and, even in spite of his luck, Paul could not bear up[107] against it. He was very anxious to see the effect of the birthday letter, telling his mother about the thousand pounds.

When there were no visitors, Paul now took his meals with his parents, as he was beyond the nursery control.[108] His mother went into town nearly every day. She had discovered that she had an odd knack[109] of sketching furs and dress materials, so she worked secretly in the studio of a friend who was the chief "artist" for the leading drapers. She drew the figures of ladies in furs and ladies in silk and sequins[110] for the newspaper advertisements. This young woman artist earned several thousand pounds a year, but Paul's mother only made several hundreds, and she was again dissatisfied. She so wanted to be first in something, and she did not succeed, even in making sketches for drapery advertisements.

---

107 bear up : 꿋꿋함을 잃지 않다, 견디다
108 beyond the nursery control : 아기방에서 지낼 나이가 넘은
109 knack : (타고난) 재주, (경험으로 익힌) 요령
110 sequin : 고대 베니스의 금화, 의복 장식으로 다는 원형의 작은 금속편

She was down to breakfast on the morning of her birthday. Paul watched her face as she read her letters. He knew the lawyer's letter. As his mother read it, her face hardened and became more expressionless. Then a cold, determined look came on her mouth. She hid the letter under the pile of others, and said not a word about it.

"Didn't you have anything nice in the post for your birthday, mother?" said Paul.

"Quite moderately nice," she said, her voice cold and absent.

She went away to town without saying more.

But in the afternoon Uncle Oscar appeared. He said Paul's mother had had a long interview with the lawyer, asking if the whole five thousand could not be advanced[111] at once, as she was in debt.

"What do you think, uncle?" said the boy.

"I leave it to you, son."

"Oh, let her have it, then! We can get some more with the other," said the boy.

---

111 advance : 선불하다, 선금으로 주다

"A bird in the hand is worth two in the bush,[112] laddie!"[113] said Uncle Oscar.

"But I'm sure to *know* for the Grand National; or the Lincolnshire; or else the Derby.[114] I'm sure to know for *one* of them," said Paul.

So Uncle Oscar signed the agreement, and Paul's mother touched the whole five thousand. Then something very curious happened. The voices in the house suddenly went mad,[115] like a chorus of frogs on a spring evening. There were certain new furnishings,[116] and Paul had a tutor. He was really going to Eton, his father's school, in the following autumn. There were flowers in the winter, and a blossoming[117] of the luxury Paul's mother had been used to. And yet the voices

---

112 A bird in the hand is worth two in the bush : <속담> 수중의 새 한 마리가 덤불 속 두 마리보다 낫다

113 laddie : 얘야, 친구 ＊ 남자아이(lad)의 애칭.

114 the Derby : 영국 경마대회의 대명사처럼 되어 있는 유명한 경마대회 ＊ 런 던 남부의 Epsom 경마장에서 열리며 가장 많은 관중이 모이는 대회로 알 려져 있음. 이 지역에서는 이 단어를 '다비'로 읽음. 앞의 Grand National 도 유명한 경마대회를 가리킴.

115 mad : 맹렬한, 격한

116 furnishings : 세간, 비품(가구, 카펫, 커튼 등)

117 blossom : (형편이) 좋아지다, 피다

in the house, behind the sprays[118] of mimosa and almond blossom, and from under the piles of iridescent cushions, simply trilled and screamed in a sort of ecstasy: "There *must* be more money! Oh-h-h; there *must* be more money. Oh, now, now-w! Now-w-w — there *must* be more money! — more than ever! More than ever!"

It frightened Paul terribly. He studied away[119] at his Latin and Greek with his tutor. But his intense[120] hours were spent with Bassett. The Grand National had gone by: he had not "known",[121] and had lost a hundred pounds. Summer was at hand. He was in agony for the Lincoln. But even for the Lincoln he didn't "know", and he lost fifty pounds. He became wild-eyed[122] and strange, as if something were going to explode in him.

"Let it alone, son! Don't you bother about it!" urged Uncle Oscar. But it was as if the boy couldn't really hear what his uncle was saying.

---

118 spray : 작은 가지
119 study away : 집을 떠나 공부하다
120 intense : 온 신경을 집중한, 진지한
121 had not "known" : 우승마를 알아맞히지 못했다는 뜻임.
122 wild-eyed : 눈이 분노에 찬, 과격한 눈매의

"I've got to know for the Derby! I've got to know for the Derby!" the child reiterated, his big blue eyes blazing with a sort of madness.

His mother noticed how overwrought[123] he was.

"You'd better go to the seaside. Wouldn't you like to go now to the seaside, instead of waiting? I think you'd better," she said, looking down at him anxiously, her heart curiously heavy because of him.

But the child lifted his uncanny blue eyes.

"I couldn't possibly[124] go before the Derby, mother!" he said. "I couldn't possibly!"

"Why not?" she said, her voice becoming heavy when she was opposed. "Why not? You can still go from the seaside to see the Derby with your Uncle Oscar, if that[125] that's what you wish. No need for you to wait here. Besides, I think you care too much about these races. It's a bad sign. My family has been a gambling family, and you won't know till you grow up how much damage it has done. But it has done damage. I shall have to send Bassett away, and ask Uncle Oscar not to talk

---

123 overwrought : 너무 긴장한, 과로의
124 couldn't possibly : 아무리 해도 ~할 수 없다
125 if that : 고작해야, 기껏해야

racing to you, unless you promise to be reasonable about it; go away to the seaside and forget it. You're all nerves!"[126]

"I'll do what you like, mother, so long as you don't send me away till after the Derby," the boy said.

"Send you away from where? Just from this house?" 5

"Yes," he said, gazing at her.

"Why, you curious child, what makes you care about this house so much, suddenly? I never knew you loved it."

He gazed at her without speaking. He had a secret within a secret,[127] something he had not divulged,[128] even to Bassett or 10 to his Uncle Oscar.

But his mother, after standing undecided and a little bit sullen[129] for some moments, said:

"Very well, then! Don't go to the seaside till after the Derby, if you don't wish it. But promise me you won't let your nerves 15 go to pieces. Promise you won't think so much about horse-racing and events, as you call them!"

"Oh, no," said the boy casually. "I won't think much about

---

126 You're all nerves! : 너는 신경이 온통 곤두서 있어!
127 a secret within a secret : 비밀 중의 비밀, 엄청난 비밀
128 divulge : (비밀을) 누설하다, 폭로하다
129 sullen : 음울한, 무뚝뚝한, 기분이 언짢은

them, mother. You needn't worry. I wouldn't worry, mother, if I were you."

"If you were me and I were you," said his mother, "I wonder what we *should* do!"

"But you know you needn't worry, mother, don't you?" the boy repeated.

"I should be awfully glad to know it," she said wearily.

"Oh, well, you *can*, you know. I mean, you *ought* to know you needn't worry," he insisted.

"Ought I? Then I'll see about it," she said.

Paul's secret of secrets was his wooden horse, that which had no name. Since he was emancipated from a nurse and a nursery-governess,[130] he had had his rocking-horse removed to his own bedroom at the top of the house.

"Surely, you're too big for a rocking-horse!" his mother had remonstrated.[131]

"Well, you see, mother, till I can have a real horse, I like to have some sort of animal about," had been his quaint[132] answer.

---

130 nursery-governess : 보모 겸 가정교사
131 remonstrate : 질책하다, 항의하다, 충고하다
132 quaint : 기이한, 기묘한

"Do you feel he keeps you company?"[133] she laughed.

"Oh yes! He's very good, he always keeps me company, when I'm there," said Paul.

So the horse, rather shabby, stood in an arrested prance[134] in the boy's bedroom.

The Derby was drawing near, and the boy grew more and more tense. He hardly heard what was spoken to him, he was very frail, and his eyes were really uncanny. His mother had sudden strange seizures[135] of uneasiness about him. Sometimes, for half an hour, she would feel a sudden anxiety about him that was almost anguish. She wanted to rush to him at once, and know he was safe.

Two nights before the Derby, she was at a big party in town, when one of her rushes of anxiety[136] about her boy, her first-born, gripped her heart till she could hardly speak. She fought with the feeling, might and main,[137] for she believed in common sense. But it was too strong. She had to leave

---

133 keep you company : 너의 친구가 되어 주다, 너의 곁에 있어 주다
134 in an arrested prance : 뛰다가 멈춘 상태로
135 seizure : (병의) 발작, (특히) 졸도 *seize : (공포, 병 등이) 덮치다, 엄습하다
136 rushes of anxiety : 엄습하는 불안감
137 might and main : 전력을 다하여, 힘껏

the dance and go downstairs to telephone to the country. The children's nursery-governess was terribly surprised and startled at being rung up in the night.

"Are the children all right, Miss Wilmot?"

⁵ "Oh yes, they are quite all right."

"Master Paul? Is he all right?"

"He went to bed as right as a trivet.[138] Shall I run up and look at him?"

"No," said Paul's mother reluctantly. "No! Don't trouble. It's

¹⁰ all right. Don't sit up.[139] We shall be home fairly soon." She did not want her son's privacy intruded upon.

"Very good," said the governess.

It was about one o'clock when Paul's mother and father drove up to their house. All was still. Paul's mother went to

¹⁵ her room and slipped off her white fur cloak. She had told her maid not to wait up[140] for her. She heard her husband downstairs, mixing a whisky and soda.[141]

---

138 as right as a trivet : <구어> 만사 순조로운, 매우 건강한, 극히 좋은
 * trivet : (철제) 삼각대, 삼발이

139 sit up : (늦게까지) 자지 않다, 앉아서 기다리다

140 wait up : <구어> 자지 않고 기다리다

141 whisky and soda : 위스키소다 * 위스키에 소다수를 탄 칵테일로 미국에서는 '하이볼'이라고 함.

And then, because of the strange anxiety at her heart, she stole[142] upstairs to her son's room. Noiselessly she went along the upper corridor. Was there a faint noise? What was it?

She stood, with arrested muscles,[143] outside his door, listening. There was a strange, heavy, and yet not loud noise. Her heart stood still. It was a soundless noise, yet rushing and powerful. Something huge, in violent, hushed[144] motion. What was it? What in God's name[145] was it? She ought to know. She felt that she knew the noise. She knew what it was.

Yet she could not place[146] it. She couldn't say what it was. And on and on it went, like a madness.

Softly, frozen with anxiety and fear, she turned the door-handle.

The room was dark. Yet in the space near the window, she heard and saw something plunging to and fro.[147] She gazed in fear and amazement.

Then suddenly she switched on the light, and saw her son, in

---

142 steal: 몰래 다가가다, 살금살금 가다
143 with arrested muscles: 꼼짝도 하지 않고
144 hushed: 소리를 낮춘, 숨죽인
145 in God's name: 도대체
146 place: 판정하다, 생각해 내다, 알아차리다
147 plunge to and fro: 앞뒤로 요동치다

his green pyjamas, madly surging[148] on the rocking-horse. The blaze of light suddenly lit him up, as he urged[149] the wooden horse, and lit her up, as she stood, blonde, in her dress of pale green and crystal, in the doorway.

"Paul!" she cried. "Whatever are you doing?"

"It's Malabar!" he screamed in a powerful, strange voice. "It's Malabar!"

His eyes blazed at her for one strange and senseless second, as he ceased urging his wooden horse. Then he fell with a crash to the ground, and she, all her tormented motherhood flooding upon her, rushed to gather him up.

But he was unconscious, and unconscious he remained, with some brain-fever.[150] He talked and tossed,[151] and his mother sat stonily[152] by his side.

"Malabar! It's Malabar! Bassett, Bassett, I know! It's Malabar!"

So the child cried, trying to get up and urge the rocking-

---

148 surge : 밀려들다, 솟아오르다
149 urge : (말 따위를) 몰아대다
150 brain-fever : 뇌염
151 toss : 잠을 뒤척이다, (아래위로) 흔들리다
152 stonily : 무표정하게, 무감각하게

horse that gave him his inspiration.

"What does he mean by Malabar?" asked the heart-frozen mother.

"I don't know," said the father stonily.

"What does he mean by Malabar?" she asked her brother Oscar.

"It's one of the horses running for the Derby," was the answer.

And, in spite of himself,[153] Oscar Cresswell spoke to Bassett, and himself put a thousand on Malabar: at fourteen to one.

The third day of the illness was critical: they were waiting for a change. The boy, with his rather long, curly hair, was tossing ceaselessly on the pillow. He neither slept nor regained consciousness, and his eyes were like blue stones. His mother sat, feeling her heart had gone, turned actually into a stone.

In the evening Oscar Cresswell did not come, but Bassett sent a message, saying could he come up for one moment, just one moment? Paul's mother was very angry at the intrusion, but on second thoughts she agreed. The boy was the same. Perhaps Bassett might bring him to consciousness.

---

153 in spite of himself: 자기도 모르게

The gardener, a shortish[154] fellow with a little brown moustache and sharp little brown eyes, tiptoed into the room, touched his imaginary cap[155] to Paul's mother, and stole to the bedside, staring with glittering, smallish eyes at the tossing,
5 dying child.

"Master Paul!" he whispered. "Master Paul! Malabar came in first all right, a clean[156] win. I did as you told me. You've made over seventy thousand pounds, you have; you've got over eighty thousand. Malabar came in all right, Master Paul."

10 "Malabar! Malabar! Did I say Malabar, mother? Did I say Malabar? Do you think I'm lucky, mother? I knew Malabar, didn't I? Over eighty thousand pounds! I call that lucky, don't you, mother? Over eighty thousand pounds! I knew, didn't I know I knew? Malabar came in all right. If I ride my horse till
15 I'm sure, then I tell you, Bassett, you can go as high as you like. Did you go for all you were worth, Bassett?"

"I went a thousand on it, Master Paul."

"I never told you, mother, that if I can ride my horse, and get there, then I'm absolutely sure — oh, absolutely! Mother, did I

---

154 shortish : 키가 좀 작은
155 touched his imaginary cap : 인사를 했다
156 clean : 흠잡을 데 없는, 완전한

ever tell you? I am lucky!"

"No, you never did," said his mother.

But the boy died in the night.

And even as[157] he lay dead, his mother heard her brother's voice saying to her: "My God, Hester, you're eighty-odd thousand[158] to the good,[159] and a poor devil[160] of a son to the bad.[161] But, poor devil, poor devil, he's best gone out of a life where he rides his rocking-horse to find a winner."

---

157 even as : ~하는 바로 그 순간에
158 eighty-odd thousand : 대략 8만 (파운드) *odd : 대략 ~의, ~남짓한
159 to the good : 이익으로
160 a poor devil : 불쌍한 놈
161 to the bad : 빚이 되어, 부족하여

작품 해설

1. "There must be more money."

이 작품의 갈등 구조는 어머니 Hester에게서 시작한다. 아름다운 외모에 또 이웃보다 훨씬 호사스런 살림살이를 유지하고 있지만, 그녀는 운이 없는 남편을 만나 인생이 망가졌다고 불만스러워하는 인물이다. 고지서는 날아드는데 돈은 늘 부족하다. Hester의 불만은 자식들과의 관계에 고스란히 전이되어 자식들에 대한 자연스러운 사랑의 감정을 그녀에게서는 찾아볼 수 없다. 문제는 1남 2녀의 아이들, 특히 아들 Paul이 본능적으로 어머니의 불만, 그로 인한 사랑의 부재를 감지하고 불안해한다는 점이다. 작가는 어머니에게서 발원하여 집안을 휩싸고 도는 불만과 불안을 환상적 설정을 통해 제시한다. "돈이 더 있어야해."(There must be more money.) 어느 순간부터 아이들은 유령처럼 온집안을 떠도는 이 신비롭고 섬뜩한 속삭임(whispering)을 끊임없이 듣게 된 것이다. 요컨대 Hester는 자본주의적 물신숭배의 광기가 체화된인물이며, 작품 초입에서부터 작가는 이 단편의 키워드가 무엇인지 노골적으로 제시하고 있다.

어머니의 불만은 아들을 불안으로 몰아간다. 그런데 아들은 신비롭게도 흔들목마(the rocking-horse)를 타고 질주하며 우승마에 대한 계시를 받고, 이를 통해 얻은 막대한 경마 수익을 제3자의 이름으로 어머니에게 전달한다. 하지만 어머니는 5년에 걸쳐 나누어 받게 될 5천 파운드에 만족하지 못하고 이를 한꺼번에 지급할 것을 요구한다. 그녀의 욕망은 충족 불가능의 괴물이 되어 더 큰 욕망, 더 집요한 탐욕으로 질주할 뿐이다. 그리고 이 탐욕은 다시 아들에게 더욱 격렬한 흔들목마 위의 질주를 요구하고 결국 Paul은 심야의 질주 끝에 죽음에 이르고 만다.

작품의 주제는 더 이상의 부연설명이 필요 없을 만큼 명쾌하다. Hester는 8만 파운드의 돈을 벌게 되었지만, 아이러니하게도 아들을 잃고 만 것이다. 물론 그 돈이 그녀를 만족시키지 못하리라는 것은 불을 보듯 뻔하다. Hester의 불만과 불안은 끝없이 질주하는 자본주의적 물신숭배의 발현이며, 이는 결국 모성 상실을 비롯한 인간관계의 파탄으로 귀결된다. 미친 듯이 질주하지만 늘 그 자리에 머물러 있는 아들의 흔들목마처럼 어머니의 욕망 역시 한없이 질주하지만 한 걸음의 성취도 이루지 못한다. 흔들목마의 질주와 어머니의 욕망 사이의 상동관계를 포착해 낸 Lawrence의 감식안에 새삼 경탄을 감출 수 없다.

2. Oedipus complex

작품 해석에 심리학이나 사회과학 이론을 기계적으로 대입하는 것만큼 어리석은 일은 없지만, 이 작품을 이해하는 데는 흥미롭게도 프로이트가 주장한 '오이디푸스 콤플렉스'가 도움을 준다. 참고로 이 내용이 포함된 프로이트의 『꿈의 해석』(The Interpretation of Dreams)이 출판된 것이 1899년이고, "The Rocking-Horse Winner"가 발표된 것은 1926년이었다.

프로이트의 주장을 간략히 요약하면 이렇다. 남근기(4~6세)에 이른 아들은 어머니의 사랑을 얻기 위해 아버지와 경쟁관계를 형성하는데, 아버지의 현실적 힘과 권위를 깨달은 후에는 거세불안이 발생하면서 아버지와의 동일시 혹은 모방으로 이 욕망을 승화시켜 성인 남자로 자연스럽게 성숙해 나간다는 것이다.

Paul은 아버지가 운이 없어 돈을 잘 벌지 못한다는 어머니의 불만을 전해 듣자 자신은 운이 있다고 큰소리를 치고 나선다. 전형적인 오이디푸스 콤플렉스의 발현에 해당한다. 잠재적 경쟁자인 아버지를 대신해서 자신이 어머니를 차지하겠다고 나선 것이다. 그리고 결국 흔들목마를 타며 얻은 영감으로 경마대회에서 거금을 손에 넣고 이를 어머니에게 전달하게 되는데, 프로이트의 해석을 따르자면 Paul의 말타기에는 성적 함의가 담겨 있으며, 질주하나 전진하지 못하는 말타기라는 점에서 생산(生産)에 이르지 못하는 성적 욕망, 곧 자위(自慰)에 가깝다고 할 수 있다.

어머니를 차지하기 위한 아들의 욕망이 비극으로 끝나는 것은 경쟁자이자 역할 모델이 되어 줄 부친의 부재 때문이기도 하지만 무엇보다도 어머니 Hester의 탐욕 탓이 더 크다. 물질적 부와 성공에 대한 그녀의 과도한 집착은 스스로를 끝없는 결핍으로 이끌고, 이는 아들의 삶에도 파멸적 결과를 초래한 것이다. 아버지의 부재로 인해 어머니가 아들에게 애착을 보이는 경우는 Lawrence의 장편소설 *Sons and Lovers*에서와 같이 어머니가 아들의 자연스러운 성장을 가로막는 장애물이 되는 경우가 많다(거기서도 주인공인 이름이 Paul이었다). 하지만 이 작품의 경우는 거꾸로 "딱딱하게 굳어 버린 가슴", 곧 누구에게도 사랑을 느끼지 못하는 어머니의 감정의 부재가 장애물이다. 정반대의 방향이지만 두 경우 모두 아들의 삶을 왜곡하고 성장을 방해한다는 점에서는 동일한 결함이라 할 수 있을 것이다. Paul이 다가오는 가을에 Eton에 입학할 계획이라는 설정으로 미루어보면 Paul의 나이는 12~13세로 추정되며, Hester 스스로 언급하듯이 이 나이는 흔들목마를 타기에는 너무 많은 나이이다. 아들을 유아기의 흔들목마에 붙잡아 둔 채 성장을 가로막은 것은 바로 어머니의 물신숭배의 광기와 굳어버린 가슴이었고, 이는 급기야 아들을 죽음으로 몰아가고 만다.